Vermillion Public Library
18 Church Street
Vermillion, SD 57069
(605) 677-7060

The Chloe and Levesque Series

Over the Edge
Double Cross
Scared to Death
Break and Enter

First American Edition 2011
Kane Miller, A Division of EDC Publishing

Copyright © 2001 by Norah McClintock.
First published by Scholastic Canada Ltd.

For information contact:
Kane Miller, A Division of EDC Publishing
PO Box 470663
Tulsa, OK 74147-0663
www.kanemiller.com
www.edcpub.com

Library of Congress Control Number: 2010933235

Printed and bound in the United States of America
1 2 3 4 5 6 7 8 9 10
ISBN: 978-1-61067-004-3

To Phil and Don,
who knew all about love and loss

Chapter 1

I opened the front door on the third ring of the doorbell and found Tessa Nixon standing on my front porch, biting her lower lip and clutching a thick binder and two textbooks to her chest as if they were armor. She peered at me with eyes as blue as a summer sky and then peeked over my shoulder, as if she expected or maybe hoped to see someone in the house behind me. She was out of luck. I was alone.

"Can I help you?" I said, after I got tired of waiting for her to speak. I felt like a counter clerk at a fast-food outlet. *Do you want fries with that?*

"I — I was wondering if maybe . . . " Her voice trailed off. She peeked over my shoulder again. Then she glanced back in the direction she had come, up at the gravel road that ran past our house. That seemed to hold her attention for a while, even though there was nothing up there except a silver-gray car that was slowing as if it were going to stop, but that in the end kept right on going.

"Uh, Tessa," I said, tapping her on the shoulder, making sure she hadn't forgotten I was there. And — I couldn't help it — I also found myself wondering why Ross had been mooning over her for the past couple of weeks. Okay, so she was pretty, although when she turned back to me her cheeks had lost their healthy, cover-girl glow. If anything,

1

the pallor gave her a damsel-in-distress look that made her seem even prettier. Besides those annoyingly blue eyes, she had skin that teenage girls the world over would have killed for, a perfect, straight nose, plump lips swept with a shade of coral lipstick that, on her, looked completely natural, and thick, shoulder-length hair that shone gold in the late afternoon sunlight. And that was just for starters. She was also tall and slim — you know, flat tummy, hint of hipbones, long legs. In her black jeans, red sweater and cropped black jacket, she looked as if she had just stepped out of the pages of a fashion magazine. But beauty is only skin deep, right? And from where I was standing, Tessa Nixon, pleasing to the eye though she was, didn't seem to have much going on upstairs. When she finally managed to turn her attention back to me, she looked a little blank, as if she couldn't remember who I was or why she was standing on my porch.

"No offense," I said, "but I have a lot of homework to do. So if you don't mind . . . " Hint, hint, Tessa.

"Your dad isn't home, is he?"

I admit it, she floored me with that one. What did Tessa want with Levesque — who, by the way, is my stepfather, not my actual father. He's also the police chief in the town of East Hastings, which I now call home.

"It's four o'clock in the afternoon," I told her.

I guess that was a little too oblique for her. She looked baffled.

"He's at work," I said, by way of clarification. If I knew Levesque, he was probably reviewing the file on the convenience store holdup that had happened ten days ago. The store's owner had been killed and the clerk, a seventeen-year-old kid, had been so seriously hurt that he was in a coma in the hospital. I could imagine Levesque poring over that file. There was nothing he hated more than an unsolved robbery-homicide. "Have you tried the police station?" I said to Tessa.

Her eyes turned all liquid, and I could imagine how Ross would have reacted if she had flashed that look at him. Here's a clue: think puddle. It didn't melt me, though. Not much, anyway.

"He'll be home this evening," I said. Then I added, "Probably," because, the fact is, you never know with cops. They're pretty much famous for not being home for dinner every day and for having to dash out in the middle of the night to attend the scene of an accident or, more likely up here in East Hastings, to arrest someone on a drunk and disorderly on a Friday or Saturday night, or to chase down some tourist who had gotten lost in the middle of East Hastings Provincial Park.

"Okay," Tessa said. Her voice was all whispery, like she was trying to be sexy or something, which, again, Ross would have lapped up like a kitten with a saucer of cream. "Okay, thanks."

She turned and started back across the porch. When she reached the steps, I swung the door shut. Then I stood there for a moment, watching her make her way down the steps, along the path to the driveway, and then up to the road. I almost opened the door again and called after her. I almost asked, "Is everything okay, Tessa?" Almost. But I didn't.

* * *

During my free period the next day, I ducked out into the schoolyard to get a breath of fresh air. The heat was still pumping through the school ventilation system, but the weather outside had forgotten how it was supposed to be behaving. It was March first, but a couple of days ago the weather had turned so warm that everyone half-expected to see trees bursting into bud. They didn't, of course, and wouldn't for another month or so. But the snow had mostly melted and everybody was strolling around with great big, goofy grins on their faces, and who could blame them? It had been a hard winter. I had shoveled more snow in the past couple of months than I had the whole time I lived in Montreal — where they have a pretty good idea how to throw winter. I'm as concerned about global warming as the next person, but I was glad to have a break from the front-walk detail.

Judging from what was going on in the school-yard, the unseasonable warmth had even sparked a little spring fever. Off to one side of the football field, Tessa Nixon and her boyfriend Jake Bailey were pressed up against each other like wallpaper and wall. They had caught everyone's attention lately with their long and loud series of lovers' quarrels.

Now it looked like they were finally making up. Good thing that Ross wasn't around to see . . .

I don't know what made me turn my head just then, but I did. That's when I saw Ross Jenkins, editor of the school newspaper and the closest thing I have to a best friend in East Hastings, standing outside one of the school exits, staring across the field at Tessa and Jake, and doing a pretty good impression of a guy whose heart has been broken into a million pieces. For a second or two, his eyes were filled with longing — I guessed he was looking at Tessa. Then longing was replaced by hate and I knew he had switched his attention to Jake.

I started toward him. I was going to slap him on the back and say something like, "What did you expect, Ross? Everyone knows she's devoted to Jake. You told me so yourself." But before I got there he wheeled around and went back into the school, and I decided that maybe there were some things that you had to figure out for yourself. In Ross's case, the problem wasn't exactly in the realm of higher mathematics. In fact, it was so two-plus-two that your average first grader would have shouted out the answer in one second flat. How come, all of a sudden, the girl of your dreams suddenly turns her back on Mr. Handsome (that's Jake and, okay, so he's also Mr. Not-Too-Bright, but then she's not exactly Ms. Brains-of-the-Universe) and starts making eyes at you? Is it because: (a) She's finally, after all those years of living across the street from you, realized that you and you alone are the man of her dreams? (b) She's having a spat with Mr. Handsome and thinks the best way to teach him a lesson is to make him jealous? or (c) Her body has been invaded by an alien life form?

Everyone — and I include in that group myself, a relative newcomer and hardly the chronicler of local matters of the heart — knew that Tessa and Jake had been going together *forever*. Everyone also knew that this particular made-in-heaven match seemed to be headed straight in the opposite direction lately. I don't know why Tessa and Jake were having problems and, frankly, I didn't care, but even I had seen them screaming at each other in the schoolyard. I had seen Tessa slam her locker shut and pirouette away from Jake. I had seen Jake slam his fist into the very same locker so hard he dented it (without even wincing — that's something you don't forget, a guy who can take that kind of pain and not even flinch). And then, out of the blue, there was Tessa with her arm linked through Ross's, and there was Ross, walking along the corridors of the school, his feet not even touching the ground. Don't get me wrong. I like Ross. He's a nice guy. But Tessa's kind of guy? Look, there's biology, but there's also chemistry. Which one produces heat and light? So I felt bad that Ross, who must have thought that he had finally (miraculously) won Tessa's heart, had to find out the hard way that he was dead wrong. And was there anything harder than seeing the girl you thought of as your very own kissing the guy you thought of as your arch-enemy? But, come on, Ross, there's real and there's make-believe. Tessa and Jake were real.

* * *

Right after school that day I headed down to the newspaper office. The East Hastings Regional High School newspaper, the *Herald*, was produced out of an office that occupied a part of the school basement, wedged in between the boiler room and the janitorial office/locker room. I was planning to beg for more time to get my newspaper article done — I had been assigned to gather and compile student opinions about the fact that now we all had to do forty hours of community service before we could graduate. Ross would be upset that I wanted more time. I don't know why. The paper didn't go to the printer until Friday afternoon. But Ross insisted that all copy, except the sports news, had to be in by Wednesday morning to give him enough time to "get it into shape." My article wasn't quite written yet. Okay, so I hadn't even started to write it. I was going to promise to deliver it to him that evening at the latest, which would mean that it could still be included in the next edition of the paper, and Ross wouldn't have to lose sleep wondering about a blank space on page three or four or whatever.

I was in a rush. I had decided to leave my announcement to the very end of lunch period so that I had a built-in excuse to duck out if Ross started to lecture me — or worse, scold me. I guess my timing explained why there were so few people in the newspaper office. In fact, there were exactly two. Ross and Tessa. Neither of them noticed when I opened the door.

Tessa's back was to me and she was shaking her head. Then she said, "I'm sorry, but I can't."

Ross was facing me, but because he was one hundred percent concentrating on Tessa, he didn't see me. Just before Tessa spoke, his face was filled with hope. It seemed to take him a heartbeat or two to process her words. Then his face sort of crumpled. You know the look, the same one you see on a little kid's face just before he starts to cry. Then Ross did something stupid — he started to beg.

"Please, Tessa? It'll be great, I promise. Please?" He looked desperate and needy — not a winning combination.

Tessa shook her head. "I can't, Ross."

"Is it Jake?" Ross said. "Is he giving you a hard time again? Is he harassing you?"

I thought about Tessa and Jake on the football field. What Jake had been doing hadn't looked like harassment to me. Ross had been there too. He had been looking at the exact same scene. Levesque always says that any cop who has ever interviewed more than one witness to the same incident knows that different people see the same thing differently. I hadn't realized until just this minute how wildly different those observations could be.

"I can talk to him, if you want," Ross said. "I can make it clear to him that you don't — "

"No," Tessa said. "It's not that. Look, Ross, I'm sorry, but I can't."

"Why not? What's the matter? Was it something I did?"

By then, even I was shaking my head. Begging and pleading were bad enough, but this was starting to sound pathetic.

Tessa mumbled something I couldn't hear, and then turned away from Ross. Ross reached out and caught her arm. He must have grabbed it harder than he had intended. Either that or he startled her, because she let out a yelp.

"Let go!" she cried.

He released her as if she were a hunk of red-hot metal. "I'm sorry," he said. "Tessa, I'm so sorry."

That's when they saw me. First her, then him. Her face turned red as she sped past me out of the newspaper office. His turned stormy.

"You ever heard of a little concept called privacy?" he snapped.

I guess I could have apologized. I could even have expressed a little sympathy at what had happened. I did neither. Instead, I decided to give him a piece of friendly advice.

"Forget about her, Ross," is what I said. "She's not your type."

If the *Herald* were the *Daily Planet* and East Hastings were Metropolis, Ross Jenkins would have been Jimmy Olsen — sweet, naïve, eager and slightly inept. An innocent, harmless sort of guy. Not a guy given to violence. But when I said what I said, a look came over Ross that surprised me. Surprised me and scared me a little. His eyes tightened, he started breathing so hard that his nostrils flared like miniature sails catching a stiff wind, and his face turned splotchy red.

"You don't know anything about this," he said. Said? Make that shouted. "This is none of your business. Stay out of my life."

I stepped back automatically because, call me crazy, but for one split second I thought meek and mild Jimmy Olsen was going to take a swing at me. Instead he rushed by me and shoved the office door open so hard that it was a miracle it didn't come off its hinges. It slammed shut again just as the bell rang, signaling the end of lunch.

* * *

The story that was going around the school by lunchtime the next day was this: Sid Talbot, who owned the local doughnut shop and who had apparently gone on a fitness craze last summer after having heart palpitations, was out jogging early that morning. I must have heard the story about two dozen times throughout the day. When kids told it, they just said, "The guy who owns the doughnut shop was out jogging." When grown-ups told it, they always took a few detours before getting to the point — you know, that it was amazing how old Sid had stuck to his daily jogging routine considering that he had spent the last twenty years doing nothing more strenuous than wiping counters and ringing up coffees and crullers. Or that it was such a coincidence that he had taken the route he had, because if the weather had been cold and if it had snowed the way it usually did this time of year, he wouldn't have been on the path that looped around the pond because you wouldn't have been able to see any path, this time of year. Stuff like that.

The shortest distance between Sid Talbot setting off on his jog and what happened was this: Sid was doing a circuit of the lake that was half-inside East Hastings Provincial Park and half-outside it. He was pounding along — he had "hit his stride," as he expressed it in a front-page article in the *East Hastings Beacon* — when he happened to glance at Elder Pond. And he thought to himself, *in all the years I've lived here, I never thought I'd see water in the pond in March, instead of ice.* That's when he saw it. That's what he said, *it:* "I wasn't even sure what it was, but I got this feeling all the same that whatever it was, it wasn't supposed to be floating in the pond like that."

The *it* turned out to be Tessa Nixon. She was dead.

Chapter 2

By noon, the cafeteria, the hallways, and the schoolyard were buzzing with the news about what had happened and how it might have happened. A fair number of girls were crying. A lot of guys looked stunned, especially the ones in Tessa's grade. Then an announcement came over the PA system, "Everyone please report to your homerooms, immediately."

Mr. Mowat was my new homeroom teacher. Since Christmas he had been subbing for Ms. Michaud, my original homeroom teacher, who was on maternity leave. Mr. Mowat was a big, burly man, a phys. ed. teacher and coach of the football team. From the reputation he had for pushing the team to championship after championship and from all the yelling and cursing he was famous for — even though, strictly speaking, he wasn't supposed to be cursing on school property or at students — he seemed like the kind of guy who would slap you hard on the back and tell you to buck up, no matter what disaster you faced. It was a shock, then, to see this big man standing in front of the class, his eyes so red and watery that it wasn't hard to imagine that he had been crying. Well, okay, so it *was* hard to imagine, but all the evidence seemed to be there. When he spoke to us, his voice sounded sort of strangled, like he was on the verge of breaking down. He held a piece of paper in one shaking hand, and he read to us from it. I found out later that all the homeroom teachers had read the exact same notice to every kid in the school. Basically, it said that there had been a terrible tragedy, that one of our fellow students had died, that there was no news yet about exactly how it had happened, and that we should all go directly home and talk to our parents. Then we were excused.

I went looking for Ross. My first stop, as always, was the newspaper office, but he wasn't there, and none of the rest of the staff had seen him all day, which was odd, since Ross practically lived at the *Herald*. Well, maybe it wasn't so odd after all. Lately, Deadline Jenkins had been preoccupied — with Tessa. When I had stopped by the office after supper the night before to drop off my article, all the lights had been on, but Ross wasn't there, even though it was Wednesday night and Ross always put in long hours on Wednesday, making sure everything was ready to go to print on Friday afternoon so that the paper would be printed and ready for distribution first thing Tuesday morning.

I checked out Ross's locker, but he wasn't there, either. Then I decided to take Mr. Mowat's advice. I decided to head home and call Ross from there.

* * *

Here's one thing I've learned as a result of living in the same house as a police detective: Crime scenes are like the nickel mines up around East Hastings — they're non-renewable resources. The police have exactly one chance to collect whatever evidence exists at the scene. That's because, no matter how careful you are, you can't enter a crime scene without somehow changing it even a little bit. If you know what to avoid and if you're really careful, you can minimize that change. But it's easier than you'd think to obliterate a footprint, to step on a critical piece of fiber so that it gets mashed and lost on the sole of your boot, to leave one of your fingerprints behind, to move something unintentionally or, worse, move it before anyone has had a chance to realize its significance. And because when you first arrive at the scene, you're not really sure what's important and what isn't, any change you make can be the change that ruins your chances of catching the criminal.

Here's something else I've learned, and no one had to tell me this. I learned it purely from observation. People are drawn to the scene of a police investigation — up here it's usually the scene of an accident investigation — the way dieters are drawn to sweets. Sure, people know that they really shouldn't indulge themselves, they know it's not good for them, they know that if they give in, it's a sign of weakness. But they just can't help themselves.

I couldn't help myself.

I had been sent home from school. We all had. There are a half-dozen routes I could have taken to get from the school to my house. Five of those routes would have taken me nowhere near the

14

pond. Guess which route I took?

Levesque must have known this would happen because not only was the scene well marked off, but its furthest perimeters were guarded by police officers I had never seen before. It turned out that Levesque had borrowed them from the Ontario Provincial Police. Good thing, too, because there must have been fifty or sixty people nearby, watching and trying to get some inside information on what had happened, what the police thought, whether Tessa's death was accidental or not. These were, needless to say, people who didn't have a good fix on Levesque. He was a by-the-book kind of guy. He never let anyone in on the progress of an investigation until he knew exactly how it was going to end, and even then you found out more about it on the news than you ever did from him.

By the time I got to the scene, there was, thankfully, no sign of Tessa. Levesque was standing with Steve Denby, one of the junior officers in East Hastings. They both had their notebooks open and seemed to be conferring about something. Steve had a camera slung around his neck, and I supposed he had been taking photos of the scene. The OPP officers were keeping people well back. I scanned the crowd. There were lots of kids, which I would have expected, but there were lots of adults, too, which I thought was kind of spooky. Adults are supposed to be role models for kids, right? So what were they doing here? What message were they sending by hanging around like a

15

pack of ghouls, eagerly awaiting the gory details? And then, of course, there was me. Standing there. Drawn there. Waiting. And hypocritically passing judgment on everyone else.

It wasn't until I turned to leave that I spotted Ross. He wasn't in among the loose group that had gravitated toward the scene and was being prevented from getting too close. Either Levesque or the OPP had already woven yellow crime-scene tape in and around the trunks of trees and out and around the path that circled the pond. Instead, Ross was far away from everyone, wandering through the scrub that ran well back from the path. His head was bent and he seemed to be looking for something. I headed toward him.

"Hey, Ross," I said. "How are you holding up?" I felt bad enough about Tessa, and I had barely known her. Ross must have felt as if his heart had just been ripped out.

He hadn't seen me coming, and jumped when I spoke.

"You okay?" I asked. "Did you drop something?"

"N-no." He glanced across to where Levesque was standing and, I'm not sure, he seemed to relax a little. I glanced in the same direction. Levesque was still deep in conversation with Steve Denby. "What are you doing here anyway?" he said.

"Same thing as everyone else, I guess. Looking." I peered at Ross's pale face. "Are you sure you're okay?"

He nodded, but looked irritated at the question.

"I'm great," he said. "Someone I've known and liked all my life is dead and no one knows why, but other than that, hey, life is terrific." He did another three-hundred-and-sixty-degree sweep of the scrub around where he was standing. Then he said, "I gotta go."

"I'll walk with you," I said. I had to say it loudly, though, because he was already striding away. He didn't answer. I thought about chasing after him. Thinking about it was as far as I got.

* * *

I was sitting on the couch in the living room, supposedly reading Act Two of *Macbeth*. Shendor, our adopted golden retriever, was lying on my feet, keeping them warm while I listened for the sound of Levesque's car crunching up the gravel driveway. When I finally heard it — which wasn't easy over Shendor's rowf-rowfing, because she had heard it first — I had to fight the urge to jump up and run to the front door to meet him. Instead, I ordered myself to stay put. I forced my eyes to run over one more page of *Macbeth*. "Is this a dagger which I see before me, the handle toward my hand?" Gripping stuff in Elizabethan England, maybe, but here in East Hastings, immediately after Tessa Nixon's death . . . well, let's just say that I had zero interest in what old Macbeth saw. Still, I forced myself to keep staring at the page I was on even after I had caught a glimpse of Levesque out of the corner of my eye, scratching Shendor behind her ears, trying to calm her down.

In fact, I didn't close the book until after he had hung up his jacket in the hall closet. Then I set the book down — what I really wanted to do was fling it clear across the room — and I stood up oh-so-casually and smiled at him. That's when he gave me that special look, the one people give you when they can tell you're about to pester them with a stupid question. It's the look that warns, "Don't ask."

But sometimes you can't help yourself. Sometimes you ask anyway. I saw the look, I asked anyway, so I guess I can't complain. I pretty much asked for it. "So," I said, "what have you found out about Tessa Nixon?"

Levesque gave Shendor a final scratch, then he stared at me with those coal-black eyes of his. If he was trying to be intimidating, it was working. Levesque is a big guy. It's not so much that he's tall — although he is that — it's more that he has a blot-out-the-sun presence, especially when he's doing a pretty fair imitation of a threatening storm cloud, which was exactly what he was doing. He was just daring me to push the issue, especially when I knew perfectly well that it was an ongoing police investigation and that he didn't talk about ongoing police investigations with anyone who wasn't carrying a police badge. He looked at me for a second longer, then turned and headed for the kitchen, where my mother was putting the finishing touches on a salad.

That left me with two choices: follow him and ask

again, or call it a day.

"Can I help you with anything, Mom?" I said, as I sauntered into the kitchen.

"You could set the table," she said. "Supper's almost ready."

I opened my mouth to protest that setting the table was Phoebe's job — Phoebe is my kid sister — but closed it fast. Getting into an argument with Mom about who does what around the house wasn't going to result in any answers. Instead, I started to pull plates and salad bowls out of the cupboard. "So," I said to Levesque, as I worked, "have they figured out yet whether Tessa's death was an accident or suicide or, well, whatever?"

My mother gave me a sharp look. Then she glanced at Levesque, who shook his head slowly.

"We're not discussing Tessa Nixon tonight or any other night," he said. "We're sticking to the rules this time, Chloe. You're going to concentrate on schoolwork and I'm going to concentrate on police work and there isn't going to be any overlap of those two areas. Do you understand?"

"Well, sure," I said, smiling, sounding perfectly reasonable. "Sure. I wasn't asking for any grisly details or anything. I was just wondering — "

He held his hand up sharply, as if he had suddenly found himself on traffic duty. You there, oncoming question, stop right this instant, you do not have the right of way.

"But — "

He shook his head.

19

"Fine," I grumbled. "Trust me, why don't you?"

"Don't forget to put out the salad dressing," my ever-helpful mother said.

* * *

Tessa Nixon had lived in East Hastings for all seventeen years of her life. She knew a lot of people and a lot of people knew her, which meant there were a lot of sad faces around school on Friday morning. It also meant that people who knew me also knew that my stepfather was chief of police. After nearly nine months in town, I actually did know a fair number of people, even if I didn't describe very many of them as close friends — I just don't seem to be built that way. And all those people wanted to know what I knew, which was exactly nothing. The ones who believed me thought I must be a real loser not to know what was going on in my own family. The ones who didn't believe me thought I was a snot for not letting them in on what I knew — which was exactly nothing.

When I went down to the newspaper office during my free period, I found Ross in his office. For the first time in all the months I had known him, his computer wasn't switched on. He was just sitting there, staring at the blank screen. He looked like a guy who had just pulled a series of pre-exam all-nighters. His face was pale. His eyes were bloodshot. He didn't even look up when I stood at his door and said, "Knock, knock."

"Go away."

"Aren't you even going to ask me what I know?" I

said.

"You don't know anything," Ross said. His voice was as flat as the prairies we had been studying in geography. "He doesn't tell you anything."

Well, okay, that was true.

"How are you feeling?" I said next.

"Go away."

"I didn't know her very well," I said, "but from what everyone is saying, she was nice."

He whirled around in his chair and fixed me with blazing eyes. "Nice?" he said, as if the word were a deadly insult. "*Nice?* For your information, she was an angel. And thanks to Jake Bailey, she's dead. He couldn't stand that she was seeing me. He harassed her. Did you know that? He harassed her and he forced her to go back to him. You know what I think? I think he knew she wasn't going to stay with him. I think that's why it happened."

"You think Jake Bailey *killed* Tessa?" Out of respect for his feelings, I tried not to sound as skeptical as I felt.

"Everyone knows he has a vicious temper. Did you see what he did to his locker two weeks ago?"

"Leaving a fist imprint in a locker isn't the same as killing your girlfriend," I said. "Even assuming she was murdered. It could have been an accident, Ross."

"If it was, we'll eventually hear about it, I guess," he said. "But I don't think that's what we're going to hear."

It turned out Ross was right.

21

Chapter 3

For the year-and-a-half that Mom has been married to Levesque, I have made a big deal about people not calling him my father — because he isn't, he's my stepfather. I've also made a big deal about people not thinking that just because he's a cop, I must have some special interest in police work or some inside knowledge about what goes on in the East Hastings Police Department. I don't. So finding out what had happened the same way everyone else did, by reading about it in the newspaper or hearing about in on the news, shouldn't have been a big deal, right?

Wrong.

On Friday evening, after supper — a supper during which Levesque had been sitting at his usual place, right opposite Mom, directly to my left, directly to Phoebe's right — I was tidying up the kitchen. Levesque had gone back to work. Mom was lying on the couch in the living room, reading the newspaper. Shendor was flopped down beside her, dozing. I had learned that that was something golden retrievers did in the ninety percent of the time they weren't eating or pestering some human to take them for a walk. I flipped on the radio, mostly to drown out the noise of Phoebe reciting, for probably the hundredth time, the speech she was giving at a public speaking competition she had entered. Just my luck, instead of music I caught the local newscast. The lead item was: "Police have ruled that the local girl found drowned in Elder Pond was a victim of foul play."

You heard it here last, folks.

Foul play meant murder. I shook my head and thought a bunch of things all at once. I thought, who could have wanted to kill Tessa Nixon? I thought about what Ross had said — that Jake had a bad temper and had been known to slam his fist into lockers, walls and maybe, at least according to Ross, Tessa. I thought about how jealousy could turn people into monsters and that maybe, despite what I had seen in the schoolyard, Tessa had dumped Jake and Jake had taken drastic action. After all, Ross had told me that Tessa was afraid of Jake.

Then, I couldn't help it, I thought about Ross. He had been crushed to see Tessa and Jake glued to each other in the schoolyard. He had also been pretty worked up the last time I had seen him and Tessa together. Love spurned can lead to some pretty strong emotions. Then I thought, get real. Ross kill someone? It was inconceivable. Still, as I scrubbed the frying pan (and wondered what my mother had against non-stick coating), a nasty little notion crept into my head. In the heat of the moment, plenty of otherwise normal people do stupid things that end up hurting other people. Ross had been upset at whatever Tessa had said to him in the newspaper office the day before she died.

She had almost jumped out of her skin when he had grabbed her. Maybe Ross had caught up with her that night. Maybe she and Ross had argued on the path that circled the pond. Maybe he had grabbed her again, innocently. Maybe she had overreacted. And maybe, because of that, something bad had happened.

I shook my head. Get a grip, I told myself firmly. This was *Ross* I was thinking about. Ross Jenkins, Honor Roll. Not Ross Jenkins, Most Wanted.

Probably the foul play was more a random-act-of-violence variety. A girl is out walking in the woods (or along a deserted road or in her own neighborhood late at night — you can pretty much name any location) and is attacked by a homicidal stranger. It happens. It happens so often in my mother's imagination that she always asks me where I'm going, what route I'm planning to take and, if I'm going to be out after dark, how I'm going to get home. Okay, so maybe Mom has a hyperactive imagination and sees a few too many bogeymen hiding in the bushes. But stuff happens, right? It even happens in places like East Hastings. It seemed likely that it had happened to Tessa Nixon.

Then I remembered something.

I dried my hands on a dish towel and grabbed my jacket from the hall closet.

"Where are you going?" my mother called to me, which, of course, woke up Shendor, who, of course, immediately started jumping up on me, begging to go for a walk. "Don't you have homework?"

"Done it," I said, which wasn't a lie if you didn't count the chemistry lab that I had to finish writing up by tomorrow morning, second period. "I promised to drop something off." I looked down at Shendor. "You can't come. Sorry, girl." Then I called to Mom, "I won't be long."

"Stay on the main roads," my mother said. "No shortcuts." Then, "How are you getting home?"

I sighed.

"I'll be careful, Mom. I promise."

The East Hastings police station sat between two banks — I always wondered which had come first, the banks or the police station — about a block from the municipal building. It wasn't a very large police department — just Levesque, a couple of junior officers, and an administrative assistant who handled phones and office stuff during the day. When I went in, the only two people in the office were Levesque and Officer Steve Denby. Steve smiled and said hi when he saw me. Levesque looked up from his computer screen and didn't smile.

"Aren't you supposed to be doing homework?" he said.

If you went by the number of times someone asked me that question, you would have thought I was some kind of slacker who went out of her way to avoid completing her assignments. I wasn't. I was doing just fine in school, thank you very much. And two could play that game.

"How's the investigation going on that convenience store robbery and murder?" I asked.

Levesque looked momentarily pained. When he thought murder, he didn't like to think unsolved.

"What can I do for you?" he said.

"I wanted to talk to you about Tessa Nixon."

Have you ever been at a friend's house and the friend says something that sounds perfectly innocent to you, but his mom or dad don't take it that way and suddenly there's tension in the air, like before a lightning storm, and you know if you had any sense at all you'd clear the room? Well, that's what Steve Denby did. As soon as he heard why I had come, he glanced at Levesque and then carried his cup of coffee into the back room.

Levesque fixed me with his dark eyes.

"I thought I made myself clear," he said. I have to give him credit — he said it nicely, as if I were a doddering old auntie who had to be reminded of her own name. "This case and every other police case are off limits to you."

"Even if I have some helpful information?"

He peered at me for a moment. I knew what that was all about. He was using his police X-ray vision to try to figure out if I really had something to say, or if this was just a pathetic attempt to wheedle some information out of him. Right. And while I'm at it, why don't I wring a few million dollars out of Scrooge McDuck?

"What information?" he said at last.

"Did Tessa come here to see you any time in the

26

last couple of days?" I asked.

His momentarily open mind shut with the resounding *clang* of a jail cell.

"That's not information, that's a question," he said. "I've already made it clear that I'm not answering any questions from civilians on this." He stood up.

I've known him for a long time now. He lives in my house. But every now and then it strikes me how much damage he could do if he ever decided to go on a rampage. He's so dense looking that he sometimes gives you the feeling he's made of solid iron. If he decided to come at you, it would be like being targeted by the biggest cannonball the world has ever seen. I stood my ground, though.

"She came to the house the other day. She wanted to see you. I told her she could probably find you here."

He didn't blink. The expression on his face didn't change. The only indication I had that he was taking me seriously was that he sat down again.

"Tessa Nixon came to the house and asked for me?"

I couldn't help it, I felt like chalking one up for the home team.

"I don't suppose she said what she wanted to talk to me about?" he said.

I shook my head. "So I guess she never came to speak with you, huh?"

"Maybe she did," he said, more to himself than to me. "Maybe I wasn't here." He pulled out his notebook and jotted a few lines. "How did she seem?"

"Seem?"

"Was she upset?"

I thought back to Tessa standing on the porch. "She seemed more nervous than upset," I said. "She kept looking over her shoulder."

"Why? Was someone watching her? Following her?"

I shook my head again. And then I remembered something else. "There was a car," I said. "A gray car. It slowed down right in front of our house." I had thought it was going to stop, but it didn't.

"Slowed down?"

"Yeah," I said. "It was gray. A sort of silvery gray. It slowed down just opposite our driveway, but it didn't stop. Tessa's face went white when she saw it."

"Did you ask her why?"

I really hated to admit it, but, "No."

"And she didn't say why it upset her?"

I shook my head again. Three shakes and you're out?

"Did you notice anything about the driver? Male, female?"

"Nothing." I hadn't even seen the driver.

"I don't suppose you got the license number?"

Again I shook my head.

"Okay," he said. "Thank you."

"Do you think it means anything?"

He gave me that look again. But, hey, you can't blame a person for trying, right?

* * *

28

I know it sounds selfish to say this, but I hate funerals. So far in my life I had been to a grand total of three. The first was for my grandmother — my mother's mother — who died when I was eight years old and whom I had never met while she was alive. Apparently she hadn't approved of the way my mother was leading her life. Too bad Grandma never got to meet Levesque. She might have changed her mind. Her funeral was a small affair in Toronto, where she had lived her whole life. Altogether maybe two dozen people had attended and none of them looked a day under eighty. Phoebe cried, mostly, I think, because she was freaked out by the open casket. Mom remained dry-eyed throughout, which surprised me. My sister Brynn, who never met our grandmother either, even though she's two years older than me, seemed stunned by the whole experience.

The second funeral I attended was for the father of Sophie LaPlante, who was my best friend up until her mother moved the family back home to Jonquière, which she did about a month after Mr. LaPlante died. Sophie's dad was a lot older than her mom. And he had heart trouble. He died out in the driveway shoveling snow one January. At Mr. LaPlante's funeral everyone cried, me included. He was a nice guy, but really I was crying for Sophie, because I knew how much she loved her dad, and I knew how jealous I had been that she had a father and I didn't. Peter Flosnick's funeral was the third. He'd taken a nose dive off MacAdam's Lookout soon after we had arrived in East Hastings. And now here I was, on my way to Tessa Nixon's funeral.

I hate funerals because I hate having to think about never seeing someone again. I hate thinking that the casket at the front of the church holds a body that used to be a person who isn't really a person anymore. I hate thinking that it — death — could happen to anyone. And I hate the weird dreams I always get after a funeral.

But you have to do the right thing. You have to pay your respects. You have to put aside your own fears and your own feelings and think about other people, like how much it would mean to Tessa's parents to have a full church and to know that their daughter had been well-liked and that she would be sorely missed. So even though I hadn't known Tessa well enough to know what her favorite color was or what she liked to do when she wasn't at school, and even if I hadn't been thinking the kindest of thoughts about her the last time I saw her — in fact, probably because of that — I went.

I think the whole school turned out that day. The principal, vice-principals and most of the teachers were there. So were all the kids in Tessa's grade and a lot of kids from other grades. There were a lot of other people there too, friends of Tessa's family, I guess. In fact, it was standing room only in the church. I bet Tessa's parents would remember that.

Ross spent the whole time glowering at Jake

Bailey, who was sitting with the Nixon family. He didn't do anything stupid, though. In fact, the only trouble that erupted involved Tessa's brother, and it was after the funeral, out of sight of Mr. and Mrs. Nixon.

The weather was still warm for early March — too warm, if you ask me, which made me think of global warming and melting ice caps and rising ocean levels. After the service was over and after the trip to the cemetery, kids drifted toward the fringes of East Hastings Provincial Park to hang out. Ross and I tagged along. Why not? Besides, nobody seemed to want to be alone.

Tessa's brother Danny was there with everyone else, which surprised me at first. I would have expected him to be home with his mom and dad. Then I thought about it. His parents had lost their daughter. Danny had lost his sister. Maybe he needed a different kind of support to get through the day.

Danny was Tessa's twin. Someone had told me that they were like characters from that book, *The Chrysalids*. They were so close that they seemed to know what the other was thinking without having to speak a single word. People are always saying things like that about twins — they have their own special communication frequency, they can read each other's minds, if one's in trouble the other knows it even though he or she is halfway around the world. I find it hard to believe, but then, I've never been a twin. Thank goodness.

Danny Nixon was as identical to his sister as a guy can be to a girl. Same blue, blue eyes, same slender build, same golden hair, which he wore shaggy. I wondered, when I saw him shamble into the park with his loser friends, whether he was going to be a comfort or a cause of distress to his parents. Danny had as much a reputation as a troublemaker as Tessa had of being an angel. And besides, he'd be a constant reminder that Tessa was dead. You couldn't *look* at him and not see Tessa.

Suddenly Ross spoke, right beside me.

"Why doesn't Levesque arrest him?" he said.

"Arrest who?" I said.

"You know who. Jake."

I studied Ross for a moment. It wouldn't have been in good taste for him to be kidding about this at this particular time, but he looked serious to me.

"There's this little procedure called collecting evidence," I said. "You know, finding something definite that links a person to the crime scene or to the crime itself. Then there's a little something called motive — "

"Jealousy," Ross said. "He was jealous because he was losing her."

"There are an awful lot of people who say that Tessa and Jake were in love."

"Are you one of those people?" Ross said. "Because if you are, you're blind."

I was going to say, no, *love* is blind, but it wouldn't have gotten me anywhere. Besides, it was right about then that someone shouted — screamed, actually. It was Danny Nixon. He was screaming at one of his friends, a weaselly guy with scrubby, too-long hair who called himself J-Boy. His real name was Jordan. Guys like him are everywhere. They're the type who are only in school because they're not sixteen yet, but the minute they are it's sayonara, see ya later, hasta la vista, baby. The fact that Danny Nixon hung around with the crew he did seemed pretty compelling proof that he hadn't surpassed his sister in the gray matter department. Another way they were twinned, I guess. Danny was screaming at Jordan, who in my opinion was a creep, but not worth wasting breath on. Then Cindy Anderson headed for Danny and tried to loop an arm through his. Cindy was Danny's girlfriend, *was* being the operative word. Not that I kept close watch on the intricacies of Danny Nixon's love life, but it was pretty hard to miss the fact that he and Cindy had broken up. I kept coming across her crying in the bathrooms at school. I think everyone kept coming across her crying in the bathrooms at school.

Anyway, Danny ignored her, and even from where I was standing I could see her eyes starting to tear up. Then one of her friends went over to her and gently tugged her away. Another of Danny's friends, a guy named Marcus Tyrell, who was eighteen and, mercifully, would be out of school at the end of this year, cuffed Jordan on the ear — cuffed him so hard he almost knocked him off his feet.

Then Marcus put his arm around Danny and started talking to him in a low voice. He led him slowly away from the crowd. Cindy kept right on crying. "I only want to help him," she sobbed. "Why does he keep pushing me away?"

I spotted Jake on the other side of the clearing. He was looking hard at Ross. Ross was looking hard right back, so I jumped into help-your-poor-friend mode and grabbed Ross's arm and started to guide him out of the park.

"He did it," Ross muttered under his breath. "I know it was him. Tessa was upset for the past couple of weeks and it was because of Jake. She was scared, Chloe."

I thought about how she had looked that day on my porch. "What do you mean, scared?"

Ross shrugged. "I don't know. Just scared. Like she was afraid something bad was going to happen."

"What?"

"I don't know," Ross said. He sounded angry and frustrated. "I asked her. I asked her a million times, but she wouldn't tell me. But it had something to do with Jake. I know it did."

I walked Ross home and told him I'd see him on Monday. But I didn't, not during the day anyway. He didn't show up at school. Then that night when I was washing the dishes I had the fright of my life. All of a sudden a face appeared in the black of the window. I dropped the platter I was holding, the one my mother loved because it had belonged to her grandmother. Luckily, I dropped it into a sink full of soapy water, so no harm was done. I retrieved it, set it into the dish drainer, then raced to the back door and said, "Ross, what are you doing out here?"

Even in the darkness I could see that something was wrong.

"I didn't want to run into your stepdad," he said.

"Why? What's up?"

"I was at the police station today," he said. "He thinks I did it."

He was kidding. He had to be kidding. "You're kidding, right?"

Ross shook his head slowly.

"They found my scarf right near where — " His voice choked off. "Right near where she was found."

Just then the moon came out from behind a cloud. It was a full moon. Perfect, I thought, because obviously the world had gone completely crazy.

Chapter 4

Ross didn't want to stay at my house because he didn't want to take the chance that Levesque would show up, so we walked into East Hastings and claimed the back booth at Stella's Famous Home Cooking. Over coffee, I prodded Ross for details.

"That's what you were looking for the day they found her, right?" I said. When I had seen him up near Elder Pond with the rest of the crowd, he'd looked like he been scouring the area for something. "Your scarf?"

He nodded.

"What was it doing near the pond?" I asked.

He wasn't looking at me when he answered. Instead he was peering down into the too-creamy surface of his coffee. "I don't know," he said.

Detection 101: When the suspect — sorry, Ross — doesn't look you in the eye when he's talking to you or answering a critical question, it generally means he isn't telling the truth, the whole truth and nothing but the truth.

"Hey, Ross, I'm over here," I said. "I'm not swimming in your coffee."

That got him to look directly at me — for about half a second. He refused to stay focused on me. Not a good sign.

"Where were you the night Tessa was murdered?" I asked. I hated to be asking the question, especially when it meant I had to watch his eyes skip back to the coffee cup, then across my shoulder toward the front of Stella's, then over to the clock on the wall, and finally settle on the salt shaker on our table.

"I was in the newspaper office," he said finally, "same as every Wednesday evening."

A cold, evil feeling crept over me.

"Anyone see you there?" I asked.

After minutes of not being able to look directly at me, suddenly he had me in clear focus. He even managed to do a fair imitation of indignation.

"You suddenly change your last name from Yan to Levesque, Chloe?"

I shook my head and gave him a sad look. "It's a good thing he hasn't asked me any questions about that night," I said.

"What's that supposed to mean?"

"You want to know where I was Wednesday night, Ross?"

I saw a strange look in his eyes. He didn't move, didn't answer, didn't even seem to breathe. "I was at the newspaper office," I told him.

If they measured emotional shocks on the Richter scale, the one Ross seemed to experience at that moment would have measured about eight-point-five. The expression on his face gave me a pretty good idea of what Anne Boleyn must have looked like just before the axe fell, or Marie Antoinette as she mounted the steps to the guillotine.

"I went by to drop off my article. All the lights were on." I paused a moment. "You weren't there."

"I — I must have been in the bathroom or something." But he looked too stunned for me to believe that the explanation was that simple.

"Did anyone see you?"

"N-no."

I stared at him for a few moments. Then I said, "You were up at the pond, weren't you? That's why they found your scarf there."

"I didn't kill her."

"So why did you just lie to me, Ross? Why did you say you were at the newspaper office when you weren't?" Even worse, I thought, if he had lied to *me*, he had almost certainly lied to Levesque. Not a good idea.

"I didn't do it," he said. He sounded as panicky as he looked. "The last time I saw Tessa, she was fine."

"You want to tell me about it?"

"What do you want to know?"

"Everything would be a good start."

He took a deep, shuddering breath.

"I know what people think," he said. "They think I'm like some pathetic peasant boy who's crazy in love with a princess he can never have." He reached for his coffee cup, but didn't lift it, didn't take a drink from it. "I guess it's true," he said. "I've always been in love with Tessa. Ever since first grade." He gave me an embarrassed, goofy sort of look. "She lives right across the street from me. And she's only five months older than me, you know. Her birthday is in November, mine is in March." We were already in March. I made a mental note to ask him exactly when his birthday was. "I always thought it was unfair. Five little months, and because of them she got to start school a year ahead of me, which all of a sudden made me a little kid and her a big kid.

"She was always nice to me, though," he continued. "She always said hi to me, even at school. Until she started going with Jake, that is, and even then it wasn't as if she stopped being nice to me. It's just that she was so involved with him, you know, and he was taking up all of her time, he was always strutting around with his arm around her." The goofy grin he had worn when he was talking about Tessa had given way to a grim expression. Then he went on. "I tried not to think about it. I went out a few times with other girls, but, I don't know, it just never worked out."

"Maybe it didn't work out because you aren't ready for anything to work out. You're only sixteen, Ross," I reminded him.

He shrugged. "Then, one Saturday a couple of weeks ago, I was out shoveling the walk, you know, after that last big snowfall we had. I looked over and I saw Tessa come out of her house. She was wearing black leggings and a red jacket, and her hair was pulled back in a pony tail. You never saw anyone look so spectacular. I figured she was on her way to hook up with Jake, but instead she came right toward me, and she said, 'Hi, Ross.'" He sounded slightly amazed. "She said, 'I guess you wish you had a snowblower, huh?' And then she said, 'So, are you doing anything special today?' I didn't know what she was talking about. I bet you anything I had a look on my face like she was talking Chinese or something." He shrugged apologetically. "Sorry."

"For what?" I said. "Have you ever heard me speak Chinese?" He shook his head. "And even if I did, why would you feel you had to apologize for mentioning it?" I don't know why I was annoyed, but I was, just like I am whenever people ask me where I'm from. So my dad was born and raised in Beijing, which makes me half-Chinese. Big deal. "Go on," I said.

"It turned out she had to drive up to Morrisville because it was her mother's birthday and she was picking up a present for her, but she was a little nervous about driving alone, you know, with all the snow, so she asked me, as a favor, if I would go with her, to keep her company. And I said yes. I wanted to ask where Jake was, why he wasn't going with her, but I thought it would jinx things if I mentioned his name. So I didn't. We drove up to Morrisville. She played music the whole time and sang along with a lot of the songs. She has a pretty voice, you know."

I bet she had the voice of an angel — at least, I'm pretty sure that's what Ross would have testified to under oath.

"We picked up the present, had some hot chocolate, then we talked and listened to music all the way back. It was the best afternoon I've had in, well, it was the best afternoon I've ever had. And then it was over and I figured that was that. She needed company and Jake wasn't around, so she asked me, but the next day everything would be back to normal, Jake would be back in the picture and I'd be out of it. Except that wasn't the end of it. Because on Monday morning, she was coming out of her house just as I was coming out of mine and she saw me and waved to me and asked me if I wanted to walk to school with her. And then when I went to the cafeteria at lunchtime, she waved me over and said she had saved a spot for me and did I want to have lunch with her. Jake was in the cafeteria. I saw him buying a sandwich and he looked over at us and didn't look happy, but Tessa didn't say anything, so I figured they must have broken up. They must have broken up and now maybe it was my time." He shook his head.

The buzz around school was that Tessa had only taken up with Ross to make Jake jealous. The consensus was that it had worked.

"I think she was afraid of him," he said.

"Did she come right out and say so?"

He shook his head. "No. But something was really bothering her. She was afraid."

He had said that before. He had also said he didn't know what she was afraid of.

"How do you know she was afraid?" I asked. "Did

she tell you?"

He shook his head. "Not exactly. But a few days before she . . . " His voice broke. He swallowed hard before continuing. "A couple of days before she died, I ran into her. It was around eight at night. I was on the way home after putting the paper to bed. It was dark and Tessa was coming toward me. She was walking really fast. When she saw me up ahead, she kind of froze. You know, the way girls do sometimes when they're out alone after dark and they see a guy coming, but they can't figure out if he's friend or foe."

I knew the feeling. It was the same one that routinely compelled my mother to ask how I was getting home after dark.

"When I was close enough and called her name and she saw it was me, she ran toward me. She threw herself into my arms." His cheeks turned a little pink with the memory. He must have thought he had died and gone to heaven. "She said she had a creepy feeling that she was being followed. I didn't see anyone, and she sort of laughed it off now that she wasn't alone anymore. But I could tell she was scared, Chloe."

I nodded.

"Then a couple of days after that, she was at school late one night, painting sets for the school play. The girls she was working with all live in the opposite direction from her, so she came down to the newspaper office to find me and ask me if I would walk her home."

"Did she tell you why?"

"No." He seemed bothered by that.

"Did she say who she thought might be following her?"

"No. But it had to be Jake."

"Tessa and Jake made up right before she died," I reminded him. "Everyone saw them together."

Ross's grip tightened on his coffee cup.

"I think she only went back to him because she was afraid of what would happen if she didn't."

"What about last Wednesday night, Ross?" That was the night she had died. "Where were you?"

He took another deep breath and looked down at his coffee again before answering.

"I ran into Tessa on my way to the newspaper office that night." Ross spent every Wednesday night at the newspaper office, making sure everything was perfect. Sometimes he was the only person in the building — if you didn't count Mr. Luckhardt, the head janitor, who seemed to practically live there.

"Ran into her?"

"Yeah. About two blocks from school."

"Was she alone?"

He nodded. "I thought that was kind of funny that she was alone after dark," he said, "you know, because she had been so afraid lately."

"Where was she going?"

"That's the thing. She wouldn't tell me. She tried to make a joke out of it. She said she was just out for a walk, but it didn't sound right. She sounded nervous."

"Maybe she was nervous because she was meeting Jake and she didn't want you to know about it because she knew it would hurt your feelings," I suggested.

"Maybe," he said. "Or maybe someone was still following her."

Not much detective work required here. "That's what you thought, right?"

He nodded.

"So you followed her?"

He hesitated a moment before nodding again. I wondered whether he appreciated the irony — there he was, following someone who was afraid she was being followed.

"And?"

"And right near Elder Pond she found out I was following her and she got really mad and told me to go away — go away and stay away. That what she was doing was none of my business."

It didn't take much imagination to see how that had stung him.

"I headed back to the newspaper office. I guess I must have dropped my scarf. But I didn't do anything to her, Chloe. She was alive when I left her. You have to believe me."

"I do," I said. "But why didn't you tell me straight out? Why did you lie?"

He looked down into his cold coffee. "People already think I'm pathetic. I didn't want everyone to think I'm a stalker, too. Besides, I didn't hurt her. I'd never hurt her."

"Okay," I said. "Come on." I put some money on the table to pay for our coffees, then I got up.

"Where are we going?"

When I told him, he shook his head.

"No way."

"You have to, Ross. It's bad enough you didn't tell the truth the first time. Come on. I'll walk you over."

Levesque looked less than thrilled to see me. But he didn't waste much eyeball time on me. Instead, he zeroed in on Ross and waited. Ross stared dumbly back. I nudged him, sharply.

He stepped forward a pace. "I think there's something I should tell you," he said to Levesque.

That was my cue to leave.

* * *

I went looking for Ross the next morning and found him staring at his locker as if it had suddenly come alive and was about to bite a chunk out of him. No wonder. Someone had taken a thick black marker and scrawled the word "Murderer" across the dull gray door. Ross stood motionless in front of it, his face so red and his eyes so watery that I thought he was going to cry. Instead, he ripped off his pullover and started to wipe at the locker door. It didn't do any good. The writing had already dried and just wouldn't come off. All he succeeded in doing was attracting attention. It's not every day you see the editor of your school newspaper, his hair standing up all over his head, frantically mopping at the door of his locker with a balled-up sweater.

"Come on," I said, tugging his arm as a crowd gathered around us. "Let's go down to the office and report this. The sooner Mr. Luckhardt hears about this, the sooner it will be gone."

Ross didn't trot along obediently. Instead, he turned all of his frustration on me.

"What did he do, broadcast it all over town?"

"Who?" I said.

"You know who," Ross answered, through gritted teeth. He was trying to make sure no one heard him, but that's pretty hard when you're growling at someone in an increasingly jam-packed corridor. "Did Levesque tell the whole world he had me in for questioning?"

"Ross . . . " I started to say, but the damage was done. Someone beside him heard what he had said and the words whispered back and through the crowd. "Nice going," I said. "What's on your career horizon? CIA?"

He wheeled away from me and ran down the hall. I watched him for a moment, then — what else could I do? — I ran after him. I didn't catch up with him until we were both shivering out beside the staff parking lot. The air had started to cool again. It would be weeks before the trees burst into bud.

"It wasn't Levesque," I told him.

His eyes narrowed. He looked as if he wanted to hit me. "Then it must have been you," he said. "I didn't tell anyone else."

"Thanks for the vote of confidence, but it wasn't me either," I informed him. "And, excuse me, but how long have you lived in this town." It was a rhetorical question. One of the first things I had discovered about Ross was that he had been born in East Hastings and had lived here every single day of his life. "This isn't exactly the secret-keeping capital of the world, Ross. You don't think it's possible that someone saw you go into the police station with your mother or with me, or saw you come out of it?"

He slumped against the chain-link fence. "Yeah," he said, "I guess." He didn't sound angry anymore. He sounded tired. Maybe even defeated. "But now everyone's going to think I did it. They're going to think I *must* have done something, otherwise why would the police question me?"

"People can think what they want. If I know Levesque, he'll get to the bottom of this and then everyone can find out just how stupid it is to jump to conclusions."

Above us on the wall, a bell rang. You don't realize how loud and annoying those bells are until you're standing directly under one. Time for homeroom. Ross gazed at the door behind us, but he didn't move.

"I've never copied off anyone's test paper," he said. "I've never used crib notes. I've hardly even skipped class. Geez, Chloe, I want to be a lawyer, you know. I know it's stupid to let it get to me like this, but what if people *believe* it? What if people think I did it? The cops don't always get it right," he said.

47

"Sometimes the wrong guy ends up behind bars."

"Well, the wrong guy never ended up behind bars on account of Levesque," I said.

Ross still didn't move.

"So," I said, long after the last bell had sounded, "I guess this blows your *hardly* record, huh?"

He looked startled and then he laughed. "There's a second time for everything," he said. Suddenly he grew serious. "Well, almost everything." The bell rang again. End of homeroom, time for first period.

"We'd better go back inside, Ross," I said, "before you completely ruin your reputation."

He nodded and pushed himself away from the wall. "Happy birthday to me," he muttered.

I felt like the world's worst friend. I should have asked him about his birthday yesterday, when he first mentioned it.

I don't know why I looked up as we opened the door to go back inside, but I did. Glaring back out at me was Danny Nixon, Tessa's twin. If looks could kill, lightning bolts would have shot out of his eyeballs and embedded themselves deep in Ross's skull.

* * *

Maybe Ross's special day improved a little after we went back into the school and maybe it didn't. But if it did, it sure didn't stay improved. At the end of the school day, as I pushed my way through a rear exit and made my way onto the field behind the school, I saw something that I hadn't seen since sixth grade. A mob of students was standing in a big circle, shouting and hooting.

"Get him!" someone called.

"Go, go, go," a chorus of someone elses chanted.

How incredibly juvenile, I thought, but there I was, heading straight for the action to find out what was going on. The last thing I expected to find was the first thing I saw.

Ross.

Ross was one of two people in the center of the howling mob. I spotted him at the exact moment that he was being punched in the stomach by Jake Bailey. Did I say punched? That makes it sound more civilized and less painful than it actually was. Jake had both of his hands clenched together — double the size, double the force — and was driving them into Ross with a motion that made him look like a lumberjack felling a tree. The effect on Ross was pretty much the same as an axe on a tree trunk, too, because when Ross caught the blow, he doubled over and toppled to the ground. Jake towered over him, while everyone around him continued howling. Then I saw Jake draw back a leg and I knew he was going to kick Ross, who was at that point writhing on the ground, clutching his stomach, his knees pulled up either to protect himself or to somehow ease the pain. I shoved my way through the mob.

"Leave him alone," I said, hoping I sounded as authoritative as a vice-principal.

That seemed to surprise Jake, at least enough to give me time to maneuver myself between him and Ross.

"Leave him alone or I'll make sure he presses charges," I said. Usually I don't like to play on the fact that Levesque is chief of police. But Ross was my friend and no one else was helping him.

"It's his fault," Jake said. His eyes were fixed on Ross and he was breathing hard. His hands were still clenched into fists.

"I don't care who started it, if you kick a guy when he's down, it's not a fair fight anymore — "

"It's his fault she's *dead*," Jake said. "He wouldn't leave her alone. He didn't want her to come back to me. She was scared of him, and when she told him she didn't want to go out with him, he did it."

Did it?

"The police even know he did it. They took him in and questioned him, didn't they? Doesn't that prove something? He killed her," Jake said. Then his voice broke and he started to sob. Big Jake Bailey, Mr. Tough-Guy, stood there in the middle of a mob out in the schoolyard and started to sob. It had a weird effect on people. First, everyone stopped talking and howling, until the only two sounds left were Jake in his grief, and Ross groaning and retching on the ground at his feet. Then someone stepped forward. Howie Moss. He was quickly joined by Dave LeMatt. I had seen them around. They were friends of Jake's. Dave put an arm around Jake's shoulders, just for a moment. Then he said, "Come on, let's get out of here." Howie and Dave, on either side of Jake, steered him out of the circle, which suddenly fell apart and then slowly drifted away.

Pretty soon Ross and I were the only ones left.

I squatted down beside him.

"You okay?"

I know, stupid question. The guy had just been beaten up and accused of murder in front of the whole school. His partly digested lunch was lying on the ground beside him. Tears were streaming down his cheeks. I dug in my backpack for some tissues, which I handed him so that he could clean himself up a little. Then I helped him to his feet.

"You want to go to the hospital?" I asked.

He shook his head. He had used up all my tissues, but his face was still wet with tears.

"She's dead," he said. "She's dead and I know he's responsible. I just *know* it."

"No one knows who's responsible yet, Ross," I said. "Come on, let's get you home."

"*He* did it. *He's* the one. He couldn't stand that she dumped him for me. He pressured her to go back. He was making her miserable."

I didn't say anything as I walked beside him. I just let him talk and cry. Get it out of his system, my mother would have called it, although, to be honest, I didn't think this was something that Ross was going to be able to shake off quickly. I walked him the four blocks to his house and made sure he went inside, then I headed home myself. The whole way back, I was doing what I bet every other kid at East Hastings Regional High was doing — wondering who really was responsible for Tessa Nixon being found face down in the pond in the mildest March on record.

Chapter 5

Ross didn't show up at school the next day. At first I was worried that he had stayed home because he was more beaten up than I'd thought. But when I went by his house after school, I discovered that wasn't the reason. Yes, one of his eyes was bruised and swollen. And, yes, he walked slowly and lowered himself down onto the sofa the way a ninety-year-old man might — cautiously, painfully, regretfully, as if he was already planning how much it was going to hurt when he had to get up again.

"My stomach's sore," he explained. I wasn't surprised, given the way Jake had plowed into him. "And my mom's mad at me because I won't press charges and I won't let her press charges."

"That's big of you, Ross," I said. I meant it. "I think Jake was just upset."

"That's not why I'm not pressing charges," he said.

I waited for an explanation. He didn't offer one. He segued right into, "He killed Tessa, you know. The sooner your stepdad realizes that and arrests him, the better."

I didn't want to talk about it. It was way too early for Ross to be jumping to conclusions and, anyway, I was convinced that his accusations about Jake weren't the result of fact or logic, but of the green-

53

eyed monster. Ross had wanted Tessa, Ross had lost Tessa to Jake, and Ross blamed Jake for that. Now that Tessa was gone, Ross wanted to blame Jake for that too. I changed the subject. Or tried to.

"How long do you have to stay home from school?"

He shrugged, then winced.

"I don't know when I'm going back," he said.

"What do you mean?"

He gave me the most withering look a person can manage when one of his eyes is half-swollen shut.

"My locker," he said.

"I passed by it today. Mr. Luckhardt has scrubbed it clean." From the look of it, he had scrubbed it with steel wool. The locker door was going to have to be repainted.

"What about all the people I've known all my life who just stood around and let Jake beat the crap out of me? I should be in a big rush to get back to school and see all of them again because . . . ?"

I could see his point. But, "It was mob mentality, Ross. People act weird when they're in a big group like that."

"They acted like they were thirsty for blood. My blood. It was *Lord of the Flies* come to life."

I had read that book last year in school, but only because I was forced to. I hadn't liked it. But I had to admit, it allowed Ross to draw a pretty good analogy.

"They'll get over it," I said.

"I'm sure *they* will," Ross said.

I don't believe I had ever heard him be quite so sarcastic. "What I mean is, they'll forget about what happened."

"Good for them."

Then something occurred to me. "Is that why you don't want to press charges?" I asked.

"What do you mean?"

Sure. It made sense. "If you press charges, the police will have to ask a lot of questions." On something like this, Steve Denby would probably end up with the assignment. He would have to talk to witnesses, to all those people who had stood around and had done nothing to stop the fight, nothing to help Ross. I could just imagine the picture that would give Steve about Ross and about Ross's so-called friends.

"I don't want to talk about it anymore," he said.

I nodded. It was bad enough the poor guy had been humiliated. On top of that, he felt betrayed by people who had known him all his life, but who hadn't stepped in when he was being beaten up. Personally, I would have taken it a lot harder than Ross. I figured this was a good time to reach into my bag of tricks.

I had made a quick detour to the Book Nook on my way over to his house. I dug into my backpack and brought out a package, which I handed to him.

"What's this?" he asked.

I shook my head. "Come on, Ross, put those investigative journalist skills of yours to work. What does it look like?" It was flat, it was rectangular in shape and it was packed inside a plastic bag on which the words *Book Nook* were emblazoned in deep blue. What did he think it was, a cactus?

He opened the bag and pulled out the book. It had seemed like the perfect gift when I saw it on the shelf, plus, when I had flipped through it, I saw it was filled with practical advice, complete with diagrams. But now, I wondered if my sense of humor was off base. Ross stared at it. Then he stared at me. Then — thank you, powers-that-be — he smiled.

"Self-defense for Dummies," he said. "Perfect."

"Happy belated birthday," I said. "Sorry I forgot."

He fixed me with his one good eye. "I bet you didn't even know it was my birthday until I mentioned it the other day."

He had me there. "Sorry about that too," I murmured.

He set the book aside. "So, what's new?"

"If you mean about Tessa, nothing that anyone has told me." And that was the truth. There's one thing that a lot of people don't know about real life as opposed to TV or the movies. In real life, police work breezes along about as quickly as, say, a glacier. Investigating takes time. Analysis of evidence takes time. Interviewing witnesses takes time. Everything takes so much time that it can drive you crazy if you happen to be someone with a burning interest in a case. It can drive you doubly crazy if you live in the same house as the person who is doing the investigating and he refuses to tell you anything, although Levesque did say, "It was good that you got Ross to come back to the station house," which I took as a compliment. The little swell of pride I felt was immediately dashed, however, when he went on to say, "You're too close to this one, Chloe. I don't want to even hear you hinting about this case until it's over, okay?"

Okay.

Except that it was like telling me, don't breathe or don't eat. How can you keep your nose out of the one thing that everyone was talking about and that your best friend was worrying about pretty much twenty-four hours a day? That's why I was glad that the phone rang almost as soon as I got home and I was offered a baby-sitting job. It would give me something else to think about.

At the same time, I was surprised by the call. The woman introduced herself as Cecily Morgan. I had never met her. I didn't even know who she was.

"I heard you do some baby-sitting," she said. "I heard you were reliable."

I felt like asking if she would repeat that to Levesque. Instead I said, "May I ask where you got my name?"

"Tessa Nixon."

Not only was I startled to hear Tessa's name, but I was astonished — and that's putting it mildly — that Tessa had told this woman something nice about me when I didn't know Tessa well and when, the last time I had seen her, I had been less than helpful. Even — this was the hardest part to admit

— a little mean.

"Once when she was sitting for me, I asked her for a few other names — you know, just in case she was ever busy. Your name was one of them. When I heard it, I remembered Terry Henderson had told me she used a sitter named Chloe, so I asked her about you." I had baby-sat a few times for the Hendersons. "Terry said you're a good sitter, very reliable."

So Tessa wasn't the one who had actually praised me. Somehow that made me feel better.

"I know this is awfully short notice, but I need a sitter for tonight. Would you be interested? I have two children. Tyler is four. Amanda is five. I won't say they're angels, but they're reasonably well-behaved."

I said yes, got her address, and promised to be at her house at seven o'clock.

* * *

Cecily Morgan lived in a log-cabin style house on a sparsely populated road that ran north from Pine Lake. She was casually dressed in a sweater and slacks, and she smelled of flowers as she ushered me into the front hall. As I pulled off my jacket I spotted Tyler and Amanda, in their pajamas and slippers, halfway up the stairs that led to the second floor. They peered shyly down at me from between the balusters. I smiled and said hi. Their hi's in return were tiny whispers.

"They may be a little quiet at first," Mrs. Morgan said, "but don't let that fool you. They're rambunc-

tious little angels, unless they're being rambunc-
tious little devils, which they promised not to be
tonight, right, guys?" She smiled at her kids and
when she did, a warm feeling seemed to radiate out
from her. "Bedtime is eight o'clock sharp," she said,
both to them and to me. Then, to me alone, "They
like a story once they're tucked in, if you don't
mind."

"I don't mind at all," I said. "I love stories."

Mrs. Morgan called them down and gave each
one a kiss and a hug. She told them to scoot along
to the TV room, which they did happily. Then she
said in a low voice, "Actually, they may be quiet a
little longer than usual tonight. We haven't been in
town for very long and the only baby-sitter they've
ever had here was Tessa. They really liked her.
They were really sad when . . . "

"I understand," I said.

She nodded and told me she'd be back no later
than ten-thirty.

The kids were adorable. We watched a half-hour of
TV together, then we played a few rounds of the
game that never dies — Snakes and Ladders. I used
to play it when I was a kid, and Mom says she did
too. Then it was time for teeth brushing and face
washing. I let them each pick out a story — they had
a pretty good collection of picture books — and I
read both. Then I settled them into their beds. They
didn't make a peep between eight and ten-thirty
when Mrs. Morgan came home, right on schedule. It
was the easiest baby-sitting job of my career.

As I pulled on my jacket, she said, "You'd better let me call a taxi for you, Chloe."

"No, it's okay," I told her. "It's a ten-minute walk home." Actually, it was more like twenty. But it would probably take that long before one of the few taxis in town showed up. Besides, Mrs. Morgan was a single mother. She probably didn't have tons of money to throw around. And truthfully, I wasn't worried about walking home. Well, not overly worried. Levesque hadn't issued a warning for females in town to take extra precautions after dark, which meant he probably suspected that Tessa's murder wasn't random. She, like most people who end up murdered, had probably known the person who had killed her. It was probably Tessa-specific, not female-general. "Besides," I told Mrs. Morgan, "it's not that late. I'll be fine."

She looked dubious. "After what happened . . . " she said.

"I'll be fine, really," I repeated.

She still looked so uneasy that I almost gave in and let her call a taxi. But I didn't. I held firm in my belief that I was perfectly safe. "If you ever need a sitter again, give me a call," I said. "The kids were great."

That brought a smile to her face. "Thanks," she said. "Good baby-sitters are hard to find." She walked me to the door. She was still standing there, illuminated by the porch light, a few minutes later when I turned the corner and her house faded from view.

* * *

It was a beautiful night. The weather had gotten a little colder again, but not as cold as you'd expect for this time of year. The air was clear and the sky was like a sheet of blue-black velvet scattered with generous handfuls of silver confetti. I still couldn't get over how many more stars you could see up here in the middle of nowhere. Back home in Montreal, you mostly saw haze and reflected light from thousands of houses, apartment buildings and office towers.

I was stumbling along toward the lake, gazing up at the sky, thinking how little I knew about what I was looking at, when, I'm not even sure why, I got this creepy feeling and all the little tiny hairs on the back of my neck stood straight up. At that exact moment I would have been willing to bet serious money that someone was following me.

I turned around, fast, to see if I could catch whoever it was in the act.

I saw . . . no one.

It's just a feeling, I told myself. You're letting your imagination get the better of you. There's a good reason why you don't see anyone following you — there *isn't* anyone following you. Remember your brilliant logic: Most murder victims were killed by someone they knew. Tessa is a murder victim, therefore Tessa was probably murdered by someone she knew. A nice, neat little package that would have been reassuring if it wasn't for that one word — probably. I started thinking of all the girls I had read about over the years who had been murdered by someone they didn't know. By lunatics, stalkers and serial killers. Suddenly a taxi started to sound like a pretty good idea. So did a cell phone. I wondered how much begging I would have to do to get one for my next birthday.

I kept walking. *Speed* walking. I would have started to run, but thinking about running made me think about grizzly bears — don't ask me why. Grizzlies just popped into my head, along with some advice I had read in an article about a woman who had survived a bear mauling. When you're face to face with a ferocious grizzly, the article had said, don't run. There's no point. A human being can't outrun a grizz. You're better off playing dead. That way you have a chance of staying alive. The woman said she had remembered that advice. She had put it into practice. But she said it was the hardest thing she had ever done, because her every instinct, not to mention every muscle in her body, had kicked into that basic human survival mode: flight.

If I started to run, I told myself, for sure I would look panicked. If I looked panicked, I further reasoned, although I'm not sure how rational I was actually being, then whoever was following me — assuming someone really *was* following me — would shift into high gear and lunge at me, and it would be game over. Better to let him think I was walking fast because I was cold than to suspect I was running because I knew he was there. But, boy, talk about the flight instinct.

He grabbed me just as I reached the loneliest stretch of the road that ran south of the highway, right before it connected with Centre Street. There wasn't a light or a house in sight. I felt his hand clamp around my elbow and, as I opened my mouth to scream, I thought, this is how Tessa must have felt.

For a split second my mind went blank. I couldn't think. I couldn't move. Then, automatically, I began to turn toward my attacker. I have no idea what was running through my mind at the time. I've heard some people, including police officers, say resistance will only enrage an attacker and lead to more serious injuries for the victim, so the best course of action is to stay calm and, please, no sudden movements. I've also read stories in the newspaper where women have ignored that advice and have fought like wild things and successfully managed to free themselves and flee to safety. I'm not sure what I was intending to do when I wrenched myself around to face whoever was holding me. I like to think I was going to fight, not fold. In the end, I did neither. I was far too stunned.

Chapter 6

I was fast getting the impression that being paranoid was common sense in East Hastings these days. If you thought someone was following you, you were probably right. If you didn't think someone was following you, you should probably think again.

"Are you out of your *mind*, Jake?" I yelled. "You scared me to death." Bad choice of words. Unless — I swallowed hard and tried to fight off the panic that swept over me.

He was still holding onto my arm, and his grip tightened until it became painful. I yelped. Then, as if he had only just realized how hard he was holding me, he let go.

"Sorry," he mumbled. "I didn't mean to hurt you. Or scare you," he added. "I just wanted to catch you alone."

Somehow, those words weren't comforting. And besides, "How did you know where to find me?"

"I called your house."

"And they told you where I was?" That didn't sound right. My mom always said it was no one's business where you were and that anyone who asked was being rude — of course, that didn't apply to *her* wanting to know where Phoebe and I were or how we were getting home. Levesque must have shared that opinion, because when someone called for Mom or Phoebe and they were out, all he ever said was, "Sorry, she isn't here right now." So, unless Phoebe . . . "Did my sister tell you where I was?"

"I told her I was a friend of yours. I said I'd borrowed your history notes and that you needed them to study." He shrugged. "She told me you were baby-sitting for Mrs. Morgan."

Thank you, Phoebe.

"What do you want, Jake?" I asked. Now that he had let go of me, I was a little less nervous. I started to walk again, and Jake didn't stop me. He fell into step beside me. Less than ten minutes was all I needed to reach the safety of the subdivision along the lake's north shore.

"I heard you were okay," Jake said.

What was that supposed to mean? "Who told you that?"

Instead of answering the question, he asked one. "Did he say anything to you about me?"

"Who?"

He looked exasperated. "Your dad."

I skipped the first-of-all-he's-not-my-dad routine — nobody ever listened anyway — and went straight to, "Why would he say anything to me about you?"

"'Cause he thinks I killed Tessa."

I didn't know Jake Bailey very well, so when I saw what looked like pain in his eyes, I couldn't tell if it came from his grief over Tessa's death or from the fact that he might be a suspect in her murder. And I didn't have any way of knowing — because a

65

certain someone was stubbornly silent on the subject — whether Jake really was a suspect or whether he was just one more possibility whose name had to be checked off the list. Civilization, in the form of houses containing people who could look out their windows and see me, was close, but not close enough yet.

"Look, Jake, my stepfather isn't in the habit of telling me anything about ongoing investigations — "

He grabbed my arm again. This time there was definitely going to be a bruise. "Don't give me that," he said. "I want to know what's going on. I have a right to know."

"Then you should be asking someone who knows," I said. "And that's not me." I jerked my arm free of his grip and started walking again.

"I didn't do it," he said.

Right. Like he would confess to me if he had.

"I loved Tessa," he said.

Some people are bad liars. Some are nervous liars. Others are over-confident liars. Sometimes, because of that, you can tell that they're lying. But Jake didn't strike me as someone who lied badly or nervously or over-confidently. Maybe he was telling the truth. Or maybe he was a champion liar. The fact was, though, that everybody said they loved Tessa, yet someone had killed her.

"I told your father I would never hurt her," Jake said. We were getting closer and closer to where the houses started. "But I don't think he believed me. My dad was there and he asked straight out if

I was a suspect."

"And?"

"Your father said he hadn't ruled anyone out yet. That's exactly what he said. Which means he suspects me, right? It's that friend of yours," he added. The words sounded bitter. "He's going around telling everyone it was me."

Levesque would never suspect Jake — if he suspected him at all — purely on Ross's say-so. There had to be another reason.

"Do you have an alibi for that night?" I asked.

"I was out in the garage. I was working on my car."

I waited. There had to be more to it than that if Jake seriously thought he was a suspect.

"My parents weren't home. They were at a bonspiel up at the curling club in Morrisville. They didn't get home until after midnight."

"What about friends?"

"I like to work alone," he said.

"Neighbors? Did you see any neighbors that night or did any neighbors see you?"

He laughed, but it was far from a cheerful sound. "Do you have any idea where I live?"

I had to admit that I didn't.

"On Ten Sideroad," he said. "Up past the cemetery."

I had been on that road more than a few times. I frowned as I tried to picture where he meant. "I didn't think there were any houses up that way," I said at last.

"You're mostly right," Jake said. "There's one house."

"Oh." So he had been alone in a remote location where no one could vouch for him. Maybe Levesque had a good reason to suspect him after all. Or maybe Jake could still look on the bright side. It depended on the answer to my next question. "Nobody can prove you weren't where you said you were, can they?"

His shoulders sagged. "The thing is, your dad has been asking questions all over town." I waited. That was, after all, his job.

"A friend of mine — a *former* friend — claims he phoned me around the time Tessa was killed. He says no one answered. So now it looks like I wasn't there."

"Don't you have voice mail, or an answering machine?"

"We had a machine," Jake said. "It stopped working a couple of months ago and my dad never got around to getting another one."

"So this friend of yours says he phoned you and the phone rang a few times and no one answered?"

Jake nodded.

"But if you were out in the garage and the phone is in the house . . . "

"There's an extension in the garage."

Oh. "Was there some reason you didn't hear the phone when it rang? Did you have a radio or CD player or something on in the car while you worked, maybe some loud music?"

He seemed to perk up for a moment. "Hey, your dad didn't ask me that," he said. "He just asked me where I was and who saw me and then a bunch of questions about exactly what I was doing to the car." He seemed quite cheerful for a split second, then his face clouded. "No," he said, shaking his head. "No, because I dropped my CD player two weeks ago — on a concrete floor. My mom was right there when I dropped it and she got really mad, like I did it on purpose or something. I totaled it." It was kind of odd, the way he said that. He reminded me of a drowning man who had finally grabbed an inflatable life preserver, only to find out that it had sprung a leak. "I told your dad, I don't care what anyone says, I never heard the phone ring."

"They can check these things out, you know, Jake," I said. "Levesque wouldn't just take your friend's word for it. He'd check with the phone company."

Now he looked alarmed. "They can really do that?"

I nodded. Some of the things you see on TV are true. Not all of them. Maybe not even most of them. But some.

"If your friend is lying, you have nothing to worry about," I said. Other than why a friend would lie when he probably knew that it would make Jake look guilty of murder. "But if your friend is telling the truth . . . " I shrugged.

"I didn't *do* it," Jake said. "I would never hurt

Tessa." He looked me right in the eye. "You have to believe me. You have to tell your dad."

Since we were already on the subject, and since it was my only chance to find out anything — Levesque sure wasn't going to enlighten me — and since Jake seemed more than willing to talk and now that he was talking, didn't seem quite so scary anymore, and since those houses were close enough now that I could run to one of them if I had to, I said, "What was going on with you and Tessa, anyway? I heard you two weren't getting along."

"You heard from that weasel friend of yours, you mean."

"Ross didn't have to tell me," I said. "I saw it with my own eyes. Everyone in school did. You and Tessa didn't exactly keep your arguments private."

He winced at the mention of her name and shook his head slowly. "I don't get it," he said. "We were going together for eighteen — no, nineteen — months. In all that time, she never criticized me. She knew I didn't care much about school. I'm not failing or anything, but it's not like I have this burning desire to go to college or be a brain surgeon."

Why do people always pick on brain surgeons in this type of conversation? Why not astrophysicists or Supreme Court justices? They're just as smart. Maybe even smarter.

"I want to be a mechanic," Jake said, with what sounded like a touch of pride and defiance. "Everyone needs mechanics, right? There isn't a computer in the world that can replace a skilled car mechanic. I'm good with engines and machines. I always have been. I like them. I understand them." He shook his head again. "I wish I could say the same about girls. For nineteen months, she liked me just the way I was. So I didn't want to be brain surgeon? So what? Then a couple of weeks ago, she started in on me — why didn't I try harder in school? Didn't I want to make something of myself? Why did I hang around with the people I did? What kind of example was I setting? Why didn't I hang around with smart people, people who had some ambition in life? She never let up. Then the next thing I know, *she's* hanging out with someone smart — Mr. Big-Deal Newspaper Editor. Like spilling a bunch of words onto a piece of paper makes one person better than another person. I couldn't figure out what had happened. So did I get mad at her? Yeah. Did I get so frustrated that I just about broke my own stupid hand pounding it into a locker? Yeah, I did. Did I want to rip the head off Ross Jenkins? You bet. But would I ever hurt Tessa? No way. I love Tessa. I'll always love Tessa."

Love, not loved. Present tense. I don't know whether he told Levesque the same story that he had just told me. If he did, I don't know what Levesque made of it. It sounded kind of convincing, though. But then, like I said, I didn't know Jake very well. For all I knew, he was a natural-born actor. "Can I ask you something, Jake?"

He nodded.

I steered around the assuming-you-didn't-kill-Tessa part and headed right for, "Who do *you* think killed her?"

The sigh that seeped out of him was long and quivery, the kind of sigh that you'd expect to hear from someone just before tears started to flow.

"Something was bothering her," he said. "Something besides me and my so-called lack of ambition, I mean. She wouldn't tell me what it was, though."

"If you had to guess . . . ?"

He shook his head. "I don't know your friend Ross all that well. I never had much time for guys like him. But he wouldn't be the first weird, little, quiet guy to snap and go homicidal."

"You think *Ross* killed her?"

"Your dad said he hadn't ruled anyone out."

Well, maybe. "Why would Ross hurt Tessa? He says he loved her too."

"Yeah, but she didn't feel the same way about him, and she told him so two days before she died." I remembered seeing Jake and Tessa kissing in the schoolyard that day. Then I remembered Tessa and Ross down in the newspaper office. "Tessa and I had had a big fight. I told her if she wanted to go out with Ross, fine, go right ahead. She told me that wasn't what she wanted. She said she was sorry for the way she'd been acting. She said she was only being friendly with him because she thought he could help her with something."

"With what?"

"She wouldn't tell me. She said it didn't matter." His voice dropped a little. "She told me she loved me. It was the last thing she ever said to me. Tell your dad that, will you? Tell him Tessa loved me and I loved her."

I said I would, mostly because I was cold and tired and wanted to go home. But I had already decided to say nothing to Levesque. First, he had made it clear that he didn't want to hear the name Tessa Nixon cross my lips — and I didn't want to hear any more lectures. Second, from what Jake had just told me about the night Tessa died, I wasn't sure where he had been and what he had been up to. If I felt that way, then for sure Levesque was looking into exactly where Jake had been and exactly what he had been doing. If that was so, then I had nothing to add. And third, Levesque had made it clear that he didn't want to hear the words Tessa Nixon cross my lips.

* * *

The sky the next morning was so filled with heavy gray clouds that the radio announcer started talking about a cold front heading our way and the possibility of snow. My mother whooped gleefully at the word snow. My mother. Whooping. Gleefully. First thing in the morning. Who says you can't be surprised by people you've known all your life? I was thinking about that on the way to school when I spotted Ross way up ahead, a few blocks from the schoolyard. At first I thought I'd have to turn on the speed to catch up with him. Then I realized that although I was walking at a leisurely pace I was quickly gaining on him. By the time I reached him across the street from school, he was at a dead stop.

"Hey, Ross," I said.

He jumped. His shoulders were bunched defensively around his ears until he realized it was me. Then he relaxed.

"You okay?" I said.

His eye wasn't as swollen as it had been the last time I had seen him, but it was still bruised. I had never seen such vivid purples and yellows clustered around a human eyeball.

He nodded, but didn't say anything. Instead, he stared across at the school as if it were a sleeping dragon that he was terrified of waking. It didn't take much brain power to figure out what was on his mind.

I looped one of my arms through one of his and kept right on walking, towing him along with me, while I said, "You know, I've been thinking about the club columns. You're right. They're only interesting to people who actually happen to be in whatever club it is." Each club in the school, from the chess club to the environment club, was entitled to space in the newspaper. It had always annoyed Ross that, by and large, those columns were badly written. "If the club secretaries wrote them differently, not only would they be interesting, but they might even help some of the smaller clubs attract more members. So I was thinking, Ross. How about if we organized a how-to session for club reporters. We could invite them all down to the newspaper office, give them a few tips and — "

"Nice try, Chloe," Ross said.

Some people say a good offense is the best defense. Personally, I find a look of pure innocence to be just as effective. "Huh? What do you mean? I was just thinking — "

"You were trying to get my mind off school, you mean," Ross said. He gave me a trembly, little smile. "I don't know what scares me more — the prospect of running into Jake again, or having to face all of my so-called friends."

I tightened my grip on his arm. "You've got two choices — drop out of school right this minute or cross the street and get on with the rest of the school year."

He stared across at the school again. His feet stopped moving.

"Come on," I said, tugging at him. "We have fifteen minutes before the bell rings. We can either put our coats in our lockers and then hide in the library until it's time for homeroom. Or we can go down to the newspaper office and find out who's on deadline and who isn't. So . . . the library or the *Herald*?"

Ross looked at me as if he couldn't quite believe his ears.

"We?" he said.

"We," I repeated. "As in, you and me."

"You and I," he corrected.

I smiled. "Spoken like a true editor, which means

we're headed for the newspaper office, huh?"

We walked arm in arm the whole way. Although he didn't try to pull away from me, I felt his muscles tense after we had crossed the street and started up the walkway to the front door of the school. A couple of people turned to look at us. A guy I knew, but not well — Mark Something-or-Other — came over and said, "You okay, Ross? I heard what happened." Ross sounded grateful as he said, "Yeah, I'm fine. It looks worse than it feels." The guy slapped Ross on the back and I bit my tongue. If Ross didn't remember seeing good old Mark in the circle that had ringed him and Jake that day, I wasn't going to remind him. Then another guy, Bob Madill, came over to us. I recognized him from the chanting mob, too. "Hey, Ross," he said. "That's some eye!"

"It sure is," Ross agreed. He touched it gingerly.

Bob sort of shuffled in front of us for a moment, blocking our way. "Hey, look," he said at last. "I'm sorry."

Ross frowned and looked confused.

"I should've done something," Bob said. "Anyone could see Jake had been in a few fights before, whereas you . . . " His voice trailed off and he shook his head. "I should have done something to stop him."

Ross blinked. Maybe it was because the sun had just come out from behind a cloud. Or maybe — more likely — it was because he realized that good old Bob had been one of the people standing on the sidelines, howling for blood.

"It's okay," Ross said. At least, that's what his voice said. His face said something else altogether. Poor Ross.

"What a jerk," I muttered when he finally got away from Bob.

"At least he apologized," Ross said. "Maybe next time something like that happens, he *will* do something."

"Maybe," I said. Call me a cynic, but I wouldn't have bet on it.

By the time we got to the newspaper office I was at least as nervous as Ross. I was trying hard to remember exactly who I had seen in the crowd, whether there had been anyone from the newspaper standing on the sidelines, watching, not helping. I couldn't remember anyone, but then I hadn't remembered Bob and Mark, either, not until they had actually come up to Ross. Then, suddenly I'd had a perfect image of their faces in the crowd.

Ross took the lead once we got to the school basement. He reached the newspaper office first and, after a split second during which his hand hesitated on the doorknob, shoved open the door. I held my breath. There was a flurry of sound inside. Then Ross was sucked into the room and hustled over to one of the desks. On it were a couple of boxes of doughnuts, some pop, juice and — a big thank you to whoever planned the party — a thermos full of coffee.

"Welcome back, Ross," said Eric Moore. Eric is

sports editor of the paper. He and Ross don't have much in common — other than a passion for news — but they still seem to be friends. There were about a dozen other kids in the office. They all crowded around Ross to ask how he was and to exclaim over what a terrible thing it must have been to be attacked like that by Jake Bailey. As far as I could tell, none of them had been there when Jake had done the deed; none of them had stood idly by while he punched and kicked poor Ross.

Those doughnuts disappeared so fast it just had to be magic. Same thing with the drinks. This time I was on the sidelines, feeling happy for Ross. His face still looked like some little kid had gone at it with a set of poster paints, but he was smiling and this time there was no effort, no pretense to it. I knew he was feeling the way I would have felt if I were in his shoes — lucky, and probably a little relieved, to find out that he had so many good friends after all.

The day must have carried on the same way as it had started, because Ross was still cheerful when I met him down in the newspaper office after classes were over. In fact, the only black spot in the day, besides the center of the bruise under one of Ross's eyes, was when we crossed the school parking lot. Jake was out there, standing beside his car. He watched us come down the walk. His fists were curled at his sides. I glanced at Ross and saw him looking over at Jake. His face was white where it wasn't yellow and purple, and I was sure he and I were thinking almost the same thing — except that where I was imagining what it would feel like to be slugged by one of Jake's hard fists, Ross was probably remembering.

I glowered across the parking lot at Jake. His eyes met mine. The only emotion I could detect was anger. The only part of him that moved was his head as he turned it to watch us go by. It wasn't until well after we had cleared the parking lot that I got up the nerve to look back to see if he was following us. Both Jake and his car were gone.

Chapter 7

Mrs. Morgan had called and asked me to baby-sit on Friday night. I wish I could have said, "I'd love to, but unfortunately I have big plans." But the truth was, I didn't — unless you want to stretch the concept of big plans to include sitting at home watching the stupid sitcoms they program for Friday nights because even television network executives know that only the most pathetic creatures in the world are actually sitting in front of the TV on Friday night. So I said yes. Might as well make a little cash while channel-surfing.

I ended up watching a kids' movie instead. Mrs. Morgan had rented a movie for Tyler and Amanda, and it was a big deal for them to stay up until nine o'clock to see the whole thing. I made popcorn — Mrs. Morgan said I could, for a special treat — and they jumped up and down excitedly when it started to poppety-pop in the microwave. I guess they weren't allowed to have it very often. I didn't mind their noisy enthusiasm, though. It was kind of cute. When they're not being total pains, little kids are pretty neat. These two had loosened up since the last time I'd seen them. They chattered happily while they ate the popcorn. They horsed around while the movie was on. And near the end, when Tyler got tired, he even snuggled up next to me. Not only did he not make a fuss when I picked him up to carry him upstairs to his bed, he actually seemed to like it. He gave me a tiny, feathery good-night kiss on my cheek, then he called a sleepy goodnight to Samantha.

"Who's Samantha?" I asked Amanda.

She yawned. Her eyes were already half-closed.

"He means Amanda," she said. "Sometimes he gets mixed up."

I tried to remember the last time I had called one of my sisters by a name that wasn't hers. Then I tried to remember being four years old. I could have called my sisters Humpty and Dumpty and I don't think I would have remembered.

I tucked in Amanda. She didn't kiss me, but she did wish me sweet dreams.

Mrs. Morgan had warned me that she was going to be home late. She wasn't kidding. It was nearly two before I heard a car pull into the driveway. I had been dozing in front of a bad movie — it was so terrible I couldn't believe that anyone had been stupid enough to actually spend a few million dollars making it. When I heard a car outside, I sat up and shook my head to try to get rid of the drowsy look I probably had on my face. When people come home that late, they probably suspect that the baby-sitter has been napping, but that doesn't mean that they want to walk in on a sitter who is sound asleep.

Mrs. Morgan had left the house alone, but she wasn't alone when she returned. She had a man with her. He stood in the front hall, nervously glancing out the window while she fumbled in her purse for money to pay me. Then Mrs. Morgan said, "Chloe, this is my friend, Tom Courtney. He'll drive you home."

Tom Courtney flashed me a smile before he glanced yet again out the little diamond-shaped window set into the front door. My stomach did a little flip. I knew Mrs. Morgan meant well. It was late and she didn't want me walking home alone. I understood that. But a thought popped into my head and I couldn't chase it out again. I couldn't help wondering if Tom Courtney had ever driven Tessa home. Driven her home and maybe . . . well . . . you know.

I must have looked as uneasy as I felt about getting a lift with Tom Courtney, because Mrs. Morgan peered at me, frowned and said, "Is everything okay?"

I smiled feebly at her and couldn't decide how to answer. I wondered if it would it be too rude to tell her what was on my mind. Then I wondered how many people had died from good manners.

Mrs. Morgan saved me from my Miss Manners moment before I had the chance to speak. "Tom, would you mind staying here with the children while I take Chloe home?"

Tom shrugged. He dropped his car keys into his jacket pocket. It was obvious that Mrs. Morgan knew him well enough to trust him with her kids, but how well placed was that trust?

"Really, I don't mind walking . . . " I started.

"It's late," Mrs. Morgan said. She sounded tired. "There is no way you're going to walk home at this hour. I can't allow it."

The only thing I could think to do was to hurry so that Tom Courtney didn't end up spending too much time alone with Tyler and Amanda. I zipped my jacket and followed Mrs. Morgan out into the driveway. That's when I noticed the car pulled up beside her battered blue Toyota. I stared at it. It was gray. Tom Courtney's car was gray. Okay, so it didn't look like exactly the same silvery gray that I remembered seeing when Tessa was standing at my front door, but the sun had been on its way down when Tessa was on my porch. It had made Tessa's blond hair look like spun gold. And I was looking at the car now under completely different conditions. Now it was lit only by the light from Mrs. Morgan's front porch. And besides, I hadn't peered at the car that had spooked Tessa as closely as I was looking at this one. I hadn't had any reason to, then. Then, Tessa had only seemed nervous for some reason I didn't understand and hadn't bothered asking about. Now, I was edging by a gray car — was it the *same* gray car? — to get to Mrs. Morgan's Toyota. Maybe I was being stupid and maybe I wasn't, but I just about went crazy when Mrs. Morgan turned out to be the slowest and most cautious driver I had ever met.

* * *

The way I heard it was this: Every February since, well, I guess since the beginning of East Hastings, the town had held a winter carnival — Winterfest. It featured snowshoe races, an ice sculpting competition, a pancake breakfast, snowmobile races, an ice fishing competition, a broom hockey tournament, "and MORE!!" as the posters around town said — all your typical winter town fun activities. And everyone in East Hastings, I heard, always turned out.

In any other year, Winterfest would have happened a couple of weeks ago. But in late January, Miles Tourley, who had for a couple of decades chaired the Winterfest committee, had a heart attack and died while stacking cases of nails in the back of his hardware store. At first the rest of the committee had been prepared to carry on, telling themselves that "Miles would have wanted it that way." But right after the funeral they discovered what the local newspaper referred to as "irregularities" in the festival's account books. Apparently old Miles had been skimming off money from the operation over the years, which probably explained how his hardware store had managed to stay open even though he hardly ever seemed to have any customers. Almost everyone shopped at the Canadian Tire just over a block away. During most of February, the newspaper was filled with articles about this scandal. There were accounts of name-calling and finger-pointing on the committee, as people accused each other of being in it with Miles. By the end of the month, though, it was proved that Miles Tourley had worked alone. The festival committee rallied. And that's how it happened that the February Winterfest was held in March that year — in the mildest March on record, as the newspaper called it.

Because of the warm weather, ice sculpting was out of the question. There were thin-ice warnings posted all along the lakeshore, so ice fishing was out too. The round-robin broom hockey tournament had to be moved from the lake to the arena. There was still some snow on the hills, but it was grainy in places, icy in others, and covered with a layer of black grit in still others, so it was an open question, closing fast, whether the toboggan races would even happen. Cross-country skiing was still on — the trees had protected enough of the snow in the park to provide ground cover. In the end it turned out that the centerpiece of this year's Winterfest wasn't the traditional winter sporting activities. Instead, it was a big block party on Centre Street on Saturday afternoon and evening. A stage had been erected and a couple of local bands recruited. There were clowns and a mediocre magician for the little kids, and plenty of stands selling hot dogs, hamburgers and french fries, even dessert sort of stuff like beaver tails and hot-waffle-and-ice-cream sandwiches. A lot of the local stores set up discount tables, and both the service club and the legion put together a few game booths — tossing hoops around pop bottles, lobbing tennis balls into fruit baskets, that sort of thing. It was all kind of lame, but this was East Hastings and it wasn't like there were a million other things to do on a Saturday afternoon, so I went. It seemed like the whole town was there, probably for the same reason.

And, okay, so it was fun. Not write-to-all-your-friends-to-boast-about-it fun, but the bands were actually pretty good, the weather was pleasant, the sky was clear, and everybody was walking around with one of those first-day-of-spring grins plastered on their faces, even though both the regional radio and TV stations were still eagerly forecasting an approaching cold front and the possibility of five to six inches of snow by the end of the week.

I picked Ross out of the crowd, over by the toss-a-tennis-ball-into-a-fruit-basket booth, and headed toward him. As soon as I got there he started to complain.

"Nothing's happening," he said. "What's taking so long? What are they doing?"

By *they*, I knew he meant the police, which, when you got right down to it, meant Levesque. I didn't have a clear idea what *they* were doing, either, but you couldn't have paid me enough to ask.

"Let's get a waffle," I said instead.

Ross shook his head. He had promised to help out at the booth, and was just waiting for his shift to begin. I left him for the waffle stand located outside the municipal building. As I was making my way through the crowd, I got the oddest feeling. I was sure someone was watching me. Staring at me, in fact. I heard once on a radio science show that there is no scientific basis for this feeling, that

another person's eyeballs don't send out special sig-
nals or anything that account for the weird feeling
you get when you're being stared at. But I felt what
I felt and I knew what I knew. I stopped and
searched the crowd. Centre Street was crammed
with people, lots of whom I either knew or recognized. But only one of them was looking at me
when I turned around. Way on the other side of the
street, his face appearing and disappearing as
people passed in front of him, was Mrs. Morgan's
friend, Tom Courtney. He was staring directly at
me. When our eyes met, he nodded and smiled, but
there was something about his smile that chilled
the warmth of the afternoon. I looked straight at
him, then dismissed him in a way that I hoped
made clear that I did not appreciate being eye-
balled by a man of his age. As I turned away, I wondered again how many times he had driven Tessa
home and if he had ever stared at her or followed
her. I wondered if I should mention these questions
to Levesque.

The waffle-and-ice-cream stand was the most
popular booth on the street. There was a crush of
people around it, but only two people actually
behind it, serving up the waffles. One of them was
Ross's mother, who worked at the municipal building. A sign propped up on the counter at her elbow
said that fifty cents from every waffle sold would
be donated to the hospital up in Morrisville, which
was running a fundraising campaign to buy some
new medical equipment. Mrs. Jenkins was moving

fast, taking orders, pulling hot waffles from the big metal container that was keeping them piping hot, and handing them over to her partner, who slapped a rectangle of ice cream between them. Mrs. Jenkins was also trying to handle the cash. The cash box sat on a counter behind her, away from the waffle-grasping hands of the crowd.

Away from all those hands, but completely unprotected. She didn't keep a good eye on it. After handing a couple of waffles to her partner, she would spin around and throw in a bill or a handful of coins and maybe grab some change, and then turn her back to it again. There looked to be quite a pile of money in the box. There also looked to be someone lurking around with more than a passing interest in it. Jordan. He was practically drooling and, if you ask me, it wasn't because of the waffles.

I got a jangly feeling as I watched him so I started to edge around the side of the stand. I glanced at the crowd behind me, and at Mrs. Jenkins and her partner. Everyone was thinking waffles and ice cream. No one was paying any attention to the money. Except Jordan.

I started to work my way farther around the side of the stand, toward the cash box and Jordan. It was slow going, though, because the crowd was so dense around me and so many little kids were trying to wriggle up closer to where the waffles were. Then I saw Jordan's hand reach out. I could imagine what he was thinking — all he had to do was dip into the cash box, pull out a handful of bills, and probably no one would even notice until the end of the day, when the cash was counted and it would seem to Mrs. Jenkins that they must have made more than that because look how many waffles they had sold.

I opened my mouth to shout a warning, when, suddenly, Jordan went sailing backward, his eyes wide with surprise, his hands, both empty, flying out behind him. It took me a moment to understand that he had been tackled by someone. I elbowed my way forward. By now everyone had turned to see what was happening. Mrs. Jenkins darted across to the back counter and grabbed the cash box before anyone could upset it. When I finally got close enough, I saw that it was Danny Nixon who had brought Jordan down. At first Danny was on top of him. Then Jordan heaved with all his might and their positions reversed — Danny was on the bottom, Jordan on top with his hand pulled back in a fist. It looked to me like he was getting ready to pound the stuffing out of Danny.

Then the cavalry arrived.

The crowd fell back like the two sides of the Red Sea and Levesque strode through, straight into the action. I saw him stand above the two boys a moment, assessing the situation. Then he leaned down and plucked Jordan off Danny. He made it look effortless, as if he were reaching down and picking up a rag doll that some little girl had dropped. Steve Denby showed up right behind Levesque and helped Danny to his feet. He and Levesque led both boys away.

* * *

"Jordan was going to steal the waffle money," I said to Levesque the next morning.

I had gotten up early — well, early for me — to write an essay that was due first thing Monday morning. Phoebe had been out since the crack of dawn. There was a big debate coming up and she was on the school's junior debating team. Mom was sleeping in. Sunday, she said, was sacred. Sunday, she stayed in bed until just before noon. Usually Levesque brought her breakfast in bed.

I almost fell over the first time I saw him climbing the stairs with a little tray on which he had put a mug of steaming coffee, a glass of grapefruit juice, a toasted bagel with smoked salmon cream cheese (Mom's favorite), and the Sunday newspaper. If you didn't know him — and even if you did — pretty much the last thing you'd ever expect to see him doing was meal delivery. He's kind of scary-looking when he's wearing his no-nonsense, police officer expression. There was nothing scary about the way he looked at Mom, though.

I was sitting on a stool in the kitchen, drinking coffee and skimming a boring book on the fur trade in early French Canada, when Levesque came back downstairs and poured himself a glass of grapefruit juice. Shendor was sleeping at my feet, although she glanced up for a moment when he entered the room. That's when I told him about the attempted robbery. I hadn't been able to get close to him after the fight and couldn't find him later, so I wasn't sure whether anyone had noticed that Jordan had been planning to steal the waffle money — I was pretty sure Danny wouldn't have told the cops — or whether, so far as Levesque was concerned, all he had been doing was breaking up a fight. From the expression on his face, I guessed it was the latter.

"Details," he said.

I had to process the word for a moment — was he dismissing what I was saying as mere details, or did he want me to tell him more?

"Danny didn't say anything about what Jordan was up to, did he?" I asked.

Levesque finished his juice, rinsed his glass and put it into the dishwasher. Then he grabbed a mug from the cupboard and poured himself a cup of black coffee. He always drank it black, no sugar. He waited for me to continue.

"I was waiting to buy a waffle," I said. "I saw Jordan eyeing the cash box. It was sitting right out there in the open. He was eyeing it and then he was moving toward it. He was going to grab money out of it, but Danny tackled him before he could take anything. Danny didn't tell you that, did he?"

"No, he didn't."

"Funny," I said.

"Ha-ha," Levesque said, although there was nothing even remotely amused-sounding in his voice.

"I mean, it's funny because you're Mr. Law-and-Order, and even though Tessa was here asking for you, she never actually went to your office to speak to you, and even though Danny knew Jordan was going to steal that money, he never actually told you. Maybe you should lighten up," I said. "Maybe you should smile more often. Then kids would tell you stuff."

Levesque has one of those big, bushy moustaches, so you can't always tell for sure, but I think he was smiling. It was one of those phony going-through-the-motions smiles, though. His eyes were somewhere else altogether. He was on the job. He was thinking. I almost said something about Tom Courtney then. Almost. But I decided not to, in the end. That would be crossing the line into an *ongoing police investigation* in great big black letters, read out in a deep, stern vice-principal voice. I drank my coffee and tried to nudge my brain along the path of the *coureurs de bois*.

Chapter 8

Mrs. Morgan called that morning while I was having breakfast. She wanted me to baby-sit for her that night. It sounded important and she apologized for the short notice. I told her, "Geez, I'd love to, but I have to go up to up Morrisville with my mother to shop for a special birthday present for my dad." Here's something I learned that morning: The vaguer you are when you tell a lie, the better it turns out. What I should have said is, geez, I'd love to, but I have something else planned. Mentioning Morrisville, my mother, and Levesque's birthday was far too specific. While it's true that being specific makes a lie sound less like a lie — details lend a little verisimilitude to the matter, as my last year's English teacher would have said — trust me, being specific is the last thing you want to be in these cases. Especially if you happen to live in the same house as a police detective.

For someone his size, Levesque can be stealthy. I know for a fact that he wasn't standing in the kitchen doorway when I picked up the phone, but he sure was there when I turned to put the receiver back in its cradle. He scared me so badly that the receiver hit the floor and bounced a couple of times before it finally made it back to where it belonged.

"I was pretty sure I told you that your mother

has her book club this evening," he said. "I'm positive that my birthday isn't until July."

My attempt at laughter was so pathetic that even Dr. Watson would have recognized it as fake.

"I guess I forgot," I said.

"Then I guess you can baby-sit for Mrs. Morgan after all," Levesque said. He picked up the receiver and held it out to me. "Why don't you call her and tell her?"

"She's probably found someone else by now."

"In the last two minutes? I don't think so." He nudged the receiver at me.

"It's okay," I said. "I don't really need the money."

"Oh." Big, long, uncomfortable pause. "And I suppose after she calls you a dozen or so more times and you make up a dozen or so excuses, she'll finally get that message, right?" Levesque was making me sound like some kind of coward, which was pretty annoying, because he had it all wrong.

"It's not that," I said.

"Then what is it?"

I hesitated. On the one hand, he had forbidden me to mention Tessa's name. On the other hand, he had asked me to explain my behavior. People shouldn't ask a question if they really don't want to know the answer. I took a deep breath and told him about Tom Courtney. To my surprise, he didn't get angry. In fact, he nodded as if what I was saying made perfect sense.

"Tom Courtney was at a convention in Toronto the day before Tessa died, the day she died, and the day after," he said. "There are dozens of people who can confirm his whereabouts."

"So he didn't do it?"

"I don't see how he could have." He nudged the receiver at me again. "It's tough being new in town," he said. "It's tough being a single mother. And it's tough to find a baby-sitter on a school night. How about it?"

I called Mrs. Morgan and told her that my mom was going to take care of the present without my help, so I could baby-sit for her after all. She was thrilled.

* * *

I guess I knew Ross would find out about Jake eventually. I guess I hoped it would be later rather than sooner. For sure I knew that you can't always get what you want.

I was in the cafeteria, looking for someplace to sit and eat the veggie wrap I had made myself for lunch. My mom's great, I love her, but to her a sandwich is something heavy on the mayonnaise that you slap between two pieces of white bread. She doesn't understand stuffed pitas or flatbread wraps. She definitely doesn't understand hummus, bean sprouts, carrot shavings or roasted red peppers.

I spotted an empty table on the far side of the crowded cafeteria — it's like there are twice as many kids as there are cafeteria seats at East Hastings Regional, which makes every lunch period like a game of musical chairs — and hurried toward it before anyone could snatch it away from me. I was halfway to my destination when I heard Ross call my name. I turned. He was a couple of rows of tables away from me, but that didn't stop him from telling me — make that *yelling* at me — what was on his mind.

"He doesn't have an alibi!" he shouted.

Almost everyone in the cafeteria stopped whatever conversation they were having so they could find out who Ross was talking about. Ross obliged them all by saying, "Jake Bailey doesn't have an alibi for the night Tessa was murdered."

I looked down at the brown paper bag in my hand. The veggie wrap it held was calling to me and I longed to answer. But it would have to wait. I reached Ross before he could say anything else, grabbed him by the elbow and steered him toward the cafeteria door. It was too late though. The damage had been done. Everyone was talking about Jake.

"What are you doing?" I asked Ross, once we were out in the relative privacy of the hall.

"Didn't you hear what I said? Jake doesn't have an alibi. He can't prove he was where he says he was the night Tessa died."

"I know," I said.

"Don't you see what that means? If he doesn't have an alibi, then he could have — " He broke off suddenly. "What do you mean, you *know*?"

"I know Jake doesn't have an alibi."

Ross peered at me. "You know because I just told

you, right?"

I could have said, "Right." I could have let him believe that was exactly what I meant. But that would have been lying. Ross was my friend. I don't think you should lie to your friends.

"I know because Jake told me."

"He *told* you?" He looked so crushed and confused that I started to have second thoughts about my not-lying-to-friends credo. "Chloe?" he prodded, when I didn't answer immediately. "Did you just say that Jake told you?"

I nodded.

"When?"

"A couple of days ago."

"And you didn't tell me?"

I took that as a rhetorical question.

Ross shook his head as if he were trying to clear it — you know, the way people do when someone has just clobbered them and they're trying to decide if all those stars they're seeing are real or concussion-induced.

"You knew Jake didn't have an alibi and you didn't tell me?" He was practically yelling now. "How come?"

"Because you would have jumped to conclusions," I said. I said it nicely, too. It wasn't my fault that he didn't take it that way.

"If I knew something that was important to you, I'd tell you," he shot back.

"I'm sorry," I said. "But now that I've told you, you're more convinced than ever that Jake did it, aren't you?" I said.

"Of course I am. You don't know Jake. You don't know what kind of temper he has. You don't know anything about his past. You don't know what Tessa told me about him."

"Which is?"

"He's not from around here, you know," Ross said.

Oh, terrific. Here comes some small town suspicion and paranoia. He's not from around here, he's not one of us; therefore, he's bad.

"Give me a break, Ross," I said.

"Jake's family only moved to East Hastings a few years ago, so a lot of people don't know about him, but I do because Tessa told me. Right before his family moved here, Jake spent a year in a group home because he was in trouble all the time. He shoplifted, he stole lunch money from other kids, he beat kids up. Then, after he got here, he got in with the wrong crowd."

"Wrong crowd?"

"You know, people like Marcus Tyrell and that creep Jordan. That bunch is always up to something and it's never something good."

"I've never seen Jake hang around with those guys," I said.

Ross ignored that. "And then there's his temper," he said. "The guy's wild. He threatened Tessa."

"Actually threatened?" I said.

Ross nodded.

That was news to me. I dragged my brain and dredged up every nasty thing Ross had said about

Jake, but this one didn't surface. "You didn't tell me that before."

"Well, he did. He told her he needed her. He told her he didn't know what he'd do if she dumped him."

Oh. "I don't know how to break this to you, Ross, but that doesn't sound like much of a threat."

"Don't you get it?" Ross said. "She was going to dump him and he couldn't take it. He says he was at home alone fixing his car, but he can't prove it. No one saw him there. No one can vouch for him. When I saw Tessa, she was scared. I bet it was Jake she was afraid of. I bet she was going to tell him she was through with him and when she did, he got angry and killed her. Who else would have wanted Tessa dead?"

"Innocent until proven guilty, Ross," I said. "Remember? He hasn't even been arrested. There are no charges against him."

"Yet."

True, but, "You didn't like it when someone wrote 'Murderer' on your locker," I reminded him.

"When *Jake* wrote 'Murderer' on my locker."

"You don't know it was him."

"*You* don't know it wasn't."

I could have pointed out that he was doing it again, he was declaring Jake guilty without any real evidence, but it wouldn't have done any good. His mind was made up.

"Leave it to the police, Ross," I advised him.

"They aren't doing anything."

"They're investigating."

Ross stared sullenly at me. I offered to share my wrap with him, but he turned me down. Then I decided to ask him something that had been bothering me ever since Jake had accosted me on my way home from Mrs. Morgan's.

"Did Tessa ask you for help with anything?" I said.

Ross frowned. "What do you mean? Why are you asking?"

"It was something Jake said."

Ross bristled at the mention of the name.

"Look, if I say anything that bothers you or hurts your feelings, it's not really me talking," I said. "I'm just repeating what Jake told me, okay?" He just stared at me. "Okay, Ross?"

Silently, he nodded.

"Jake says Tessa — " I hesitated, searching for the right way to put it. In the end, I chose abbreviation and left out the parts that might cause Ross pain or offense. "He says Tessa told him that she wanted your help with something."

Ross blinked. This seemed to be news to him.

"Why would he say that?" he said.

"I don't know. So she didn't ask you for any kind of help?"

He shook his head slowly.

"She didn't ask you for anything at all?"

A funny look washed over his face, and I knew he was remembering something. But he shrugged, as if dismissing whatever it was.

"What, Ross?" I prodded.

"Nothing."

"She didn't ask you for something — or about something?"

Still he hesitated. Then he frowned again. "Well," he said slowly, "she did ask me about you."

I guess I should have been flattered. Instead, I was baffled. "Me? What did she want to know about me?"

"She wanted to know what you were like."

She did? "Did she say why?"

He shook his head. "I thought she was just being curious."

And I thought, sure, that's why your cheeks are pink again. "Come on, Ross, what did you really think?" I asked.

He looked down at the floor. "Okay, so I thought maybe she was jealous. I thought maybe she had seen us around school together and she wanted to know if I was going out with you."

I didn't laugh. I didn't even crack a smile. Ross wasn't the type of guy I would ever go out with, but I liked him. I liked him a lot.

"Do you think that's what she really meant?" I asked.

He sighed. "No, I guess not. She wanted to know what kind of person you were. She said she'd heard you were really smart — you know, because of what happened with Peter and with Jonah."

Peter Flosnick had had a fatal fall. So had Jonah Shackleton's mother. And even though it had looked like case closed on both deaths to most people, it hadn't been. I had gotten myself all mixed up in finding out what had really happened to them, and earned myself a reputation as sort of a sleuth — or, in Levesque's mind, a meddler.

"Tessa was curious about Levesque, too," Ross said.

"Curious? What do you mean?"

"She wanted to know what he was like. Is he nice, is he fair, or is he one of those cops who think everyone is hiding something and who especially won't give kids a break."

She must have liked what she heard from Ross, because just before she died, Tessa had been on my front porch looking for Levesque. But why? And why hadn't she gone down to the police station to find him? Ross was no help — he hadn't even known she'd come to the house.

* * *

I had the feeling Ross was still mad at me for talking to Jake and not telling him about it, but I went looking for him after school anyway. When I found him I offered to walk home with him.

"You don't have to," he said, by which I knew he meant he didn't want to walk home with a back-stabbing, secret-keeping traitor of an ex-friend like me.

"Sure I do," I said. "Even when you're mad at me, Ross, you're still my friend."

One thing about Ross: He has a good heart. I think that's why he relented, although he did say,

"I would have told *you*, you know."

"I know," I said, because I knew he would have. Then I changed the subject. "So, whatever happened to that special supplement you were planning on environmental activism in the region?" Ross was a big supporter of environmental groups. He was always telling me that everything is interconnected to everything else, and that especially up here, where mining and logging were big industries, people need to be especially aware of environmental issues and what was going on around them so that they could protect their environment.

"I'm still working on it," Ross said. "As a matter of fact . . . "

And he was off. Slowly at first, then picking up speed, going on about what he had planned so far and how maybe it would be a good idea to tie the supplement into a Green Day at school, maybe the newspaper and the school environment club could bring in representatives from a couple of environmental groups to talk to the kids. Hey, maybe we could even get David Suzuki to pay us a visit — you never know until you try, right? It was pure good old Ross, a nice change from the last few days. Too bad it didn't last all the way home.

We were maybe half a block from where Ross and I normally part company when, out of nowhere, Jake appeared. He ignored me and walked straight to Ross, right up close to him. My mom, who is very big on personal space, would have called it invading his territory.

"What's the matter with you?" Jake said. He yelled the words, which, considering that he and Ross were almost joined at the nose, was almost comical. I didn't laugh, though. "You get your kicks telling lies about people?"

Ross's face had gone pale as Jake spoke and he leaned away from Jake a little, but he stood his ground.

"I never lie," he said. "All I said was, you don't have an alibi for the night Tessa was killed. You don't, do you?"

I don't know who noticed them first, Ross or me. I'm pretty sure we turned in unison. I don't know what sparked it for Ross, but for me it was a flash of movement that I caught out of the corner of my eye. Standing on the other side of the road, watching, listening, grinning, but not in a cheery way, were Marcus Tyrell and Jordan. Ross's face turned a shade paler.

"Brought your friends along with you, huh?" he said to Jake. There was a tremor in his voice. Maybe he was remembering what it had felt like to be punched hard in the stomach.

Jake glanced across the street. He saw and then seemed to immediately dismiss Marcus and Jordan.

"Those guys aren't my friends," he said. "They haven't been my friends for a long time. Besides, I don't need anyone to fight my fights for me. I can handle myself."

Judging from the way color continued to fade from Ross's face, I think he took that as a threat. In

fact, if he lost any more color he would be trans-
parent.

"Is that what you're going to do?" he said to Jake.
I noticed that tremor in his voice again, which
meant that Jake must have noticed it, too. "You're
going to fight me?"

Jake snorted. "I guess after what I did to you, I
pretty much deserve whatever I get. But I *didn't*
hurt Tessa and I *don't* appreciate you telling everyone that I did." With that, he turned and strode
away.

Ross slumped against me. Maybe he couldn't
believe Jake had just walked away. I could hardly
believe it myself. "You okay?" I asked.

He murmured something I didn't catch. It took a
few moments for him to pull himself together so
that we could continue our walk to his house.
When we parted company, I stood at the end of his
driveway and watched him walk to his front door.
He kept glancing back over his shoulder. I guess he
was still nervous.

I waited until he was inside, then headed off
toward the park to take the scenic route the rest of
the way home.

Chapter 9

I don't mind walking with other people, but a lot of times I like to be alone. So I was kind of glad when Ross and I parted company. Looping around and through the park would give me time to think, time to decompress. Walking and solitude are, in fact, a great combination.

I turned off on the gravel road that rings the west side of East Hastings Provincial Park and started to saunter through the southeast end of the park. I had been walking for about five minutes when a man stepped out onto the road about fifty yards in front of me. No big deal. The provincial park is a park, after all, which means that it attracts all kinds of people, a lot of whom like to walk along the gravel road and enjoy the sights, sounds and smells of nature. Since it wasn't dark, it didn't bother me.

It didn't bother me, that is, until I got close to the guy and noticed that he was looking at me a little too intently, like he was trying to commit my face to memory. Either that or he was trying to place me. Whichever it was, it was unnerving. I stepped up my pace and didn't look directly at him. Instead, I concentrated on the trees — the evergreens and the never-in-winter-greens — as if they were the sole reason I had taken this route. Out of the corner of my eye, I saw that the stranger and I were on a collision course, and, I'm not sure why, but I found myself wishing that I had taken another route or that I had already passed him and was out of sight so that I could start running. It probably had something to do with Tessa. Hmmm, park, all alone, stranger, danger . . . make that, it definitely had something to do with Tessa.

The man got closer and closer and then, instead of stepping aside and walking around me, he came right up to me and blocked my path.

"Excuse me," he said.

No, excuse *me*, but my whole life is passing before my eyes.

"I guess you don't recognize me, but I've seen you around," he said. If this was supposed to put me at ease, it didn't work. "You've been at my house, baby-sitting," he said. "I'm Andrew Morgan Tyler and Amanda's father." He smiled at me. Something in his eyes made me think that he was trying hard to look non-threatening. He must have heard about what had happened to Tessa. He must have known that every teenage girl who was accosted by a strange man in the park was either going to scream or run, or maybe both, and, assuming she left the park in one piece, was going to tell her parents about the incident.

I shook my head slowly. I was thinking, if you're their father and if you've seen me around, how come I haven't seen you? Trouble was, I couldn't decide whether this would be a smart thing to say, or a stupid one.

"My wife and I are divorced," he added, and grinned sort of stupidly, as if he were embarrassed to have to admit this.

I didn't say anything. I waited. I was dying — and, believe me, I was also hoping I wasn't going to end up meaning that literally — to know why Tyler and Amanda's daddy had chosen a gravel road in East Hastings Provincial Park as the appropriate place to introduce himself to me. And the harder he tried to look harmless, the more nervous he appeared. Not a good sign, if you ask me.

"Look," he said, "the thing is, when my wife and I split up, she was pretty mad at me. The way it ended up, she got more or less complete custody of the kids. I get to see them for a couple of days at Christmas and for two weeks in the summer, and that's it. How can anyone have a decent relationship with their kids when they only get to see them for a grand total of three weeks in the whole year?"

A mildly interesting question, I thought, and one that had exactly what to do with me? I glanced around, half-hoping that I would see a police cruiser coming down the road toward me. Okay, so maybe I was *desperately* hoping.

"Look," Andrew Morgan said, "here's the thing. I'm in the process of taking my wife to court to try to get joint custody. I'm the kids' father, after all." So he had said. "I know you've been baby-sitting for my wife." Right. He had seen me around. A less than comforting thought. "And I could use some help, if you know what I mean." I didn't. "I'm not

asking you to do anything illegal. I'm not even asking you to do anything wrong. I'm just asking for
help."

Help? What kind of help, I wondered.

"You don't have to answer right away. I just want
you to think it over. I love my children. They're
great little kids, aren't they?" He got that soft
daddy look on his face and, I couldn't help it, I
smiled. They *were* great kids. "All I want is the
right to see them more often. And you can help me.
You can give me some information about how my
wife is raising them — whether they seem happy,
whether they have everything they need, whether
they're being properly looked after, who she's asso-
ciating with and what kind of effect they have on
the kids. That's all I'm asking. Think it over, okay?
Think it over and let me know. If you don't want to
help me, that's fine. Really. But I love those kids
and I don't know what I'll do if I can't see them
more often. It's not fair that I have to be cut off
from them just because my wife and I didn't get
along." He shrugged and looked pretty sad.
"Please," he said, "just think it over. And if you
decide, man, this guy must be nuts, there's no way
I'm going to help him, that's okay. I know I must
sound like some kind of lunatic. Just do me one
favor? Don't tell my wife about this. Don't make it
harder for me. Okay?"

He stepped aside to let me pass. I looked at him
a moment longer, then I circled around him and
walked with what I hoped looked like a normal,

un-scared, modest pace. I walked all the way home without looking back to see if he was following me.

I didn't tell Mrs. Morgan that night that I had run into her ex-husband in the park. I thought about it, though. I thought maybe she'd like to know that her good old ex had asked me to spy on her. Then I thought, wait a minute, you don't know anything about these people. Maybe there's a good reason they don't share custody of their children. For example, maybe he's a rotten father who walked out on the family and he didn't decide he wanted the kids until after she made good and sure he couldn't get them. That happens. Or maybe he cheated on her and it was a bad divorce and she decided to use the kids to get even with him for dumping her. That happens too. Judging by what you read in newspaper advice columns, all kinds of things happen all the time. Those same advice columns also tell you that, generally, the best thing to do with the lives of people you barely know is to stay out of them. Mind your own business. Let nature take its course.

So I baby-sat for Tyler and Amanda for a couple of hours after supper, kept my mouth shut when I collected my money from Mrs. Morgan when she got home, and then I went home and enjoyed the rest of the evening. That is, I enjoyed it as much as a person could who had a history essay due third period the next day and who had done only preliminary reading on the topic — in other words, who hadn't yet put fingers to keyboard to pound out a first draft. So, actually, I spent most of the night, into the wee small hours, thinking about something I hope I don't have to spend any time thinking about ever again — the fur trade in seventeenth-century French Canada and the *coureurs de bois* who carried on that trade. It was a relief when the next morning rolled around. I was eager to get to school and drop my essay on Mr. Lawry's desk. Mind you, I would have been eager to go anywhere, to the dentist, to prison even, so long as I wouldn't run into a *coureur de bois* while I was there.

* * *

East Hastings Regional High School puts out a newspaper, the *Herald*. The *Herald* gets read. Mostly it gets read because anyone picking it up can be pretty much guaranteed to see something in it that mentions someone they know — a member of one of the sports teams, someone in one of the school clubs, someone who has won a contest or written an article or who has a band or an act in the annual school variety show. There's something in the *Herald* for everyone's inner gossip and newshound.

But getting read doesn't usually mean getting grabbed up within the first ten minutes of school on Tuesday morning. Nor does it usually mean that you can walk into school and see every single student with a copy in his or her hands, and all of them talking about what they were reading in it. Even major dailies don't get that lucky.

So you can imagine my surprise when I sailed

through the front door of the school and saw the halls clogged with chattering, *Herald*-reading students. I would have picked up a copy of the paper myself to see what they were wound up about, but the cardboard boxes at the front door that usually held the *Herald* on Tuesday morning were all empty. I glanced around and finally spotted Phoebe in a knot of her friends. Normally I make sure to keep a good mile or so between Phoebe and me during school hours, but today she had something I wanted. I elbowed my way over to where she was standing and grabbed the *Herald* from her.

"Hey!" she howled.

"I'll give it right back," I said. "I just — "

Holy Libel Laws, Batman! I stared at the lead article on page one — an article which I had seen in draft form last week — and wondered how Jake Bailey's name had gotten mixed in with a story about the school district's decision to cut funding to the girls' athletic program in order to make sure that our championship-winning boys' football team had the resources it needed to keep right on winning championships. The last time I had seen that article it had been headlined, "Football Scores at Expense of Girls' Soccer." The article I was looking at now read, "Killer on the Loose at East Hastings Regional."

"Has he lost his mind?" I said aloud.

"Do you think Dad knows?" Phoebe asked. She called Levesque Dad. Once in a rare while I referred to him in the same way but, if you ask me, it never came out sounding natural. I like him a lot, but he isn't my dad. If I have to call him anything, I call him Louis, which he doesn't mind. When I think of him, though, I think of him as Levesque.

I didn't have time to answer Phoebe's question, not that I was necessarily going to, because all of a sudden a battalion of teachers swept down the hall, led by the two vice-principals. I couldn't catch their words above all the babble, but I had no trouble understanding what they were up to. They were appropriating each and every copy of the *Herald*. I'm not a huge fan of vice-principals, but I have to say that I might have done the same thing if I'd been in their shoes. I might have been right there with them, snatching papers out of students' hands.

Mr. Mowat, my homeroom teacher, was one of the teachers on grab duty. He was practically tearing papers out of kids' hands. I watched as he reached out to snatch another one, but something funny happened. All of a sudden his hand dropped away, leaving this particular newspaper in the hands of the kid who was holding it. It was Danny Nixon. He was holding tightly to his copy of the *Herald*. Mr. Mowat looked at Mr. Moore, one of the vice-principals. Mr. Moore nodded. Danny got to keep his paper. I sort of understood, but only sort of.

It occurred to me that if they were confiscating the paper, then something — like say, the roof — was probably going to fall in on Ross. The natural place for this to happen was the principal's office, so that's where I headed, folding my copy of the *Herald* under my jacket so that no one would try to take it from me.

Ross was sitting on the bench just inside the administration office, waiting, I guessed, for Ms. Jeffries, who I could see through the glass wall that gave her a good view of the goings-on in the whole office. Ms. Jeffries was talking on the phone. I took a seat on the bench next to Ross and asked him more or less the same question I had asked my sister. "Are you out of your mind, Ross?"

He stiffened and looked defiantly at me. "You mean because I dared to tell the truth?"

"I mean because you're an idiot," I said. It sounded a little harsh, but I was stunned by what he had done. Stunned and angry because I knew he was going to land in big trouble. "How would you like it if you told someone a secret about your life and that someone told someone else who then decided to plaster it all over the front page of the newspaper?"

That's exactly what Ross had done. He had written and printed an article that told the whole school the secrets that Tessa Nixon had told Ross about Jake — namely, that Jake had been in trouble before he moved to East Hastings, exactly what that trouble had been (and it was all according to Tessa — there was no mention of any other source that verified anything in the article) and that because of that trouble, Jake had spent time in a group home.

"It's the truth," Ross said. His chin jutted out in a

way that made him look unattractively stubborn.

"It's also the truth that you took a teddy bear to bed every night until you were ten years old," I said. I knew because I had overheard his mother talking to my mother at the Canadian Tire checkout one day. "Would you like me to feature that on page one of the *Herald*?"

Ross's stubbornness was shoved aside by a look of embarrassment.

"That's — "

" — different?" I said, finishing his protest for him. "You bet it is. Because if I did that, it wouldn't be illegal, whereas what you've done is. Which, by the way, isn't the smartest move for someone whose big dream is law school."

He was shaking his head before I finished speaking. "If you're talking about libel, you're wrong," he said. "I didn't say anything in that article that isn't true."

"I'm talking about the Young Offenders Act," I informed him. "Newspapers can't name people who are charged under the Young Offenders Act. It's against the law. And despite what some people think, the *Herald* is a newspaper."

For the first time since I had joined him on the bench, Ross looked nervous.

"I just wanted people to know," he said.

"Know what? That Jake messed up when he was thirteen? That — "

A shadow fell across me. Ms. Jeffries's shadow.

"Ross," she said, "please come into my office. You

and I need to have a little discussion."

Mr. Defiance looked like Mr. Jelly-Legs as he got up and followed Ms. Jeffries down the short hall to her office. I watched through the big window. Ross sat down facing Ms. Jeffries's desk. Ms. Jeffries sat down behind the desk. Then she got up again and crossed to the window. She looked directly at me, then lowered the blind, blocking my view of what was going on. I got the message.

I decided to wait for Ross out in the hall, but he was still in the office when the homeroom bell rang. I had to duck into the girls' bathroom to wait so I wouldn't get tagged and sent to class by one of the roving vice-principals.

When Ross finally emerged I scooted out of the bathroom and chased him down the hall. "What happened?" I asked.

His eyes were red when he looked at me. Either he had been crying or he was trying hard not to.

"I got suspended," he said. "Three days, effective immediately. And it's going on my permanent record."

Ross's whole life was geared to generating a perfect permanent record by getting straight A's, by staying out of trouble, and by being involved in enough of the more intellectually oriented extracurricular activities — the debating team, the newspaper, the chess club — so that he'd be a shoo-in for the university and law school of his choice. Breaking the law in high school was probably not the best way to make a good first impression on the legal profession. Too bad he hadn't thought of that sooner.

I walked him to his locker, helped him gather his books, and then I walked him to the front door of the school and said I'd call him later. I felt sorry for him, even if the trouble he was in was his own stupid fault. And about the crying — I finally decided that he had been crying a little already and that he'd probably cry a lot more once he was home alone in his room.

* * *

Speaking of crying . . . I popped into the second floor girls' bathroom after chemistry, my last class of the day. The place was empty, which was no surprise, because I had stayed late in class to finish writing up a lab. I didn't hit the bathroom until twenty minutes after the last bell had rung, which was about nineteen minutes after everyone else had either left the school or reported to one of the extra-curricular activities that existed in abundance at East Hastings Regional. As I was standing at the sink, washing my hands and wondering if it was time for a haircut, I heard a snuffling sound. I glanced around. The door of the cubicle nearest the windows was closed, but I didn't need X-ray vision to know that someone was in there and that she was crying.

I washed my hands and dried them, then I headed for the door. In the end, though, I turned back to the windows and said, "Are you okay in there?"

The crying stopped abruptly, as if whoever was in there had just realized that she was not alone. A nice little act, I thought, but I wasn't buying it. I mean, come on. I had run water in the sink. I had dried my hands under one of those hot-air hand dryers, a first-generation piece of equipment that roared like a vacuum cleaner. And *now* Miss Tears was so embarrassed to be caught weeping that she suddenly shut up?

"Cindy, is that you?" I called through the door.

There was a moment of silence before a small, mouse-like voice said, "Yes." I heard a *phwump-phwump* sound, and knew she was pulling sheets of that horrible rough toilet paper from the little metal dispenser inside. The cubicle door opened and Cindy Anderson came out, dabbing at her eyes.

I didn't know her very well. In fact, my knowledge of her could be summed up in four sentences. She sat two rows over in my French class and couldn't have conjugated a regular -*er* verb even if her life depended on it. She was on the cheerleading squad. She had, until recently, been going out with Danny Nixon. And if she didn't stop crying about her break-up with Danny pretty soon, she was going to dehydrate. Normally I don't dispense advice to people I know as slightly as I knew Cindy. But in her case, and on behalf of every female student in East Hastings Regional, I felt I had to say something.

"He's not worth crying yourself into a prune over," I told her.

"But I love him."

"I bet he isn't in the boys' bathroom crying over you."

"You don't understand," she said, blubbering

again. "He needs someone to talk to, especially now. Tessa used to look after him. Who's going to look after him now?"

"He dumped you, Cindy. I could be wrong, but that sounds to me like his way of saying he doesn't want you to look after him."

Look out, here comes Niagara Falls.

"Look," I said, when there was a break in the deluge, "you seem like a nice person. A sensitive person." Far too sensitive. "You should pull yourself together. It doesn't do any good to spend weeks crying in the bathroom. Danny doesn't care. It's not going to get him back. All it does is make you look like someone who can't even think straight without a boyfriend glued to her. Is that really what you want people to think?"

As a tear-dryer, my little speech worked like a charm. As a pal-maker, however, it was a bust.

"Who asked you, anyway? This is my private life. It has nothing to do with you." She strode toward the door.

"If you want to keep your private life private," I shouted after her, "you should keep it out of public bathrooms."

Atta girl, Chloe. How to make friends and influence people. I'm so good at it, I could write a book on the subject.

* * *

Tuesday night. A pile of homework. Three more days of school ahead of me before the weekend, and a couple of essay deadlines, rolled around. The only consolation was that I had the place to myself. Mom had gone to the movies with a couple of the "girls" from work. If they were girls, then I was still a baby. Phoebe was at a friend's house, supposedly doing schoolwork, but I had serious doubts. I had overheard her talking to her friend and suspected that it was a boy project, not a school project, that was in the works — unless, of course, they had added lip liner and eyebrow plucking to the curriculum while I wasn't looking. Levesque was — where else? — at the police station. Shendor was dozing in her basket in the kitchen.

I don't mind doing my homework in my room. It's a good-sized room, reasonably well equipped. But I prefer to turn on the stereo and stretch out on the big couch in the living room. Now that's the way to study.

I loaded the CD player with disks and settled down to a series of math problems, followed by questions on a novel we were reading in French. I would never have told Mom or Levesque, but I actually enjoyed myself. Under the right conditions, which includes good music, a mug of sugary tea and extreme comfort, homework is not so bad.

It was after nine by the time I closed all my books and stuffed them into my backpack so that they would be ready for the next morning. I carried my mug into the kitchen and put it in the dishwasher — a habit I had picked up after my mom took to dragging me out of my room, even out of bed, to make me carry mugs and plates that I had left in the living room back into the kitchen.

"Geez, what's the big deal?" I complained, whenever she went on one of those rampages.

"If it's not a big deal, then you shouldn't mind cleaning up after yourself," she said mildly. She could be diabolically logical.

After I put everything away I headed for the stairs, planning to take a bath before bed. I don't know what made me go to the front door. It was a clear night, and I remember glancing at the little window in the door and seeing the moon low in the sky so that it seemed to be lying on the Evanses' roof across the road. I went to the window to take a good look, and that's when I saw him standing out there. Standing and staring at our house.

At first I was startled. Then I was baffled. I shoved my feet into my sneakers, grabbed my jacket from the hall closet and headed out into the night to ask Danny Nixon why he had staked out our house.

He was standing across the road, leaning against the trunk of a big, leafless maple. I was sure he was staring at our house, which meant that he would have seen me walking up our long gravel driveway and then crossing over to him. But when I finally reached him, it seemed to take a while for his eyes to zero in on me and for him to recognize me. The reason why wasn't a mystery. I could smell him from at least two yards away. Danny Nixon, age sixteen, had been drinking.

"Hi, Danny," I said.

He gave me a crooked little smile, which, on him, was attractive. I began to understand why Cindy Anderson was always crying in the bathroom.

"You find something interesting about my house?" I said.

He shook his head.

"Then what are you doing here?"

He shrugged. "Just wondering."

"About anything in particular?"

"No."

He shoved himself away from the tree he had been leaning on. He didn't say anything as he started to walk away. He was weaving a little as he faded into the darkness. I watched him until he vanished, and wondered what had he been looking for. What, or who.

Chapter 10

The next day after school, I walked over to Ross's house to give him his homework assignments. It was the least I could do. His mother answered the door. She looked relieved to see me and ushered me in, saying, "Ross will be glad you're here."

I wasn't so sure about that. After all, I had called him an idiot the last time I had seen him. But whatever I had said was said and couldn't be taken back, so I drew in a deep breath and headed down the stairs to the basement.

Ross was sprawled on a couch in front of a big-screen TV. Granted, the TV wasn't on and his history textbook, not *TV Guide*, was propped up on his chest. He wasn't studying, though. Instead, he was staring out into space. Then he heard me. He blinked and turned his head, but he didn't say anything right away. I wondered if he was still mad at me.

"I brought your homework assignments," I said. "I figured you wouldn't want to fall behind."

He shrugged. At least I think it was a shrug. It's hard to make out specific gestures when the person making them is lying down and is half hidden by *Modern World History*.

I handed him the sheet of paper on which I had written the assignments I'd collected from his teachers. Then I sat down on a chair near the couch. "You okay?" I asked.

"I guess." He sighed. He wrestled himself into a sitting position and set the history book aside. "Is Jake being investigated?"

"I have no idea, Ross." Of course, he knew that already. Or he should have known. "I heard he was pretty upset about what you wrote in the newspaper, though." The rumor going around was that tears of anger and frustration had been seen on Jake's face. That, plus he had tried to put his fist through a wall in the locker room. Only it turned out the wall wasn't drywall, it was concrete, so guess who had to be taken to the hospital? I didn't tell Ross, though. I couldn't decide whether it would have made him feel better or worse if he knew Jake had hurt himself, and I knew I'd get angry all over again if he seemed glad.

"My mother thinks I should apologize to him," Ross said.

"Oh?" I didn't know Mrs. Jenkins well, but she sounded like she had a lot in common with my mother. "Are you going to?"

Ross stared at the floor for a few moments. Then he looked up at me. "Someone killed her, you know, and I can't think of a single person besides Jake who had a good reason to. That's why I did what I did — to show everybody that there's another side to Jake Bailey. Will I apologize to him? If it helps to clear my record, yes, I'll tell him I'm sorry about writing the article — I'm sorry it got me suspended. I'll even tell him I didn't show good judgment, because that's true, too, and it could turn out to hurt me in the long run. But I'm not sorry if what I did hurt Jake or embarrassed him or made him feel bad."

I could have argued with him, but it wouldn't have done any good. Besides, I hadn't come here to get into another fight.

"Ross, are you sure you can't think of any reason why Tessa might have wanted to talk to Levesque?" That had been bothering me for days. I'd be sitting in my room, working on a French essay or studying for a history quiz, and suddenly I'd see Tessa Nixon standing on my porch, clutching her textbooks to her chest, looking nervous and asking if Levesque was home. If only I had asked her what was wrong. If only I had pressed her for details.

Ross gave me a who's-an-idiot-now look.

"Maybe she wanted to tell him she was afraid of Jake," he said. "Jake who, by the way, doesn't have an alibi for the night Tessa died."

Jake who, if he wasn't where he told me he'd been, had lied to me. But why? Why would he go to all the trouble of catching up to me near the lake that night to tell me something that wasn't true? I had no influence over anything, so why bother? It didn't make sense. And what about Danny Nixon? Why had I found him standing in front of my house, staring at it as if it contained the secrets of the universe? I guess if you want to talk turkey, you go and see a turkey farmer, right?

* * *

The Nixons lived across the street from Ross, in one

of the older, nicer houses in East Hastings, a big, square white house with a porch that wrapped around all four sides. The trim was painted dark green, the house surrounded by an expanse of landscaped lawn. It was the kind of house that I used to look at in picture books when I was a kid back in Montreal, when we lived in a third-floor apartment a few blocks east of Mont Royal, one of those places where you have to climb up two flights of metal stairs on the outside of the building. In winter, when those stairs are slicked over with ice, they're treacherous. Back then I'd look at my picture books and see houses that looked like they were made out of gingerbread, with lush green yards all around them and huge trees with swings hanging from them, and I'd think how I'd give everything I had, even my sisters, if I could live in a house like that.

I stood on the sidewalk, staring up at the Nixons' house. Coming over here had seemed like a great idea. All I had to do was march up to Danny and ask him why he had been at my house and if he had any idea why Tessa had been there. But now here I was, staring at the house and remembering that the people who lived in it had recently lost their daughter. Mr. Nixon worked at the Ministry of Natural Resources, so maybe he was home and maybe he wasn't. But I knew for a fact that Mrs. Nixon didn't work. She was probably inside. She might even be crying. Did I really want to walk up there and ring her doorbell?

It turned out I didn't have to. As I stood hesitating, the front door opened and out came Danny. He was pulling on his jacket as he came down the steps and didn't even notice me. I don't think he saw me until he was practically nose to nose with me. Then he stared at me as if I were a four-eyed giant carrot or something — like, what is this alien life form doing on my property? His eyes were unfocused. I was beginning to form an unflattering picture of Danny Nixon's spare time activities.

"Hi," I said.

He grinned at me. "Hey, I know you," he said. "You're the cop's kid, right?"

I took another look at him and decided he probably wouldn't care about the difference between a stepfather and a biological father. "What were you doing at my house last night?" I asked.

He looked confused. "Was I at your house?"

"You were standing across the street, staring at it."

"Oh," he said. He shrugged. "I don't remember." He started to circle around me.

"Your sister was at my house just before she died," I said.

That stopped him dead. But when he turned back to me, he was still smiling.

"Yeah? I didn't know you were friends with my sister."

"I wasn't." I let him think about that for a moment, then I said, "She didn't tell you?"

He didn't bite. I hate it when you try to bluff someone and not only do they not fall for it, they don't even lean a little.

I shook my head. "I'm surprised," I said, trying to sound downright astonished. "If she didn't tell you she was going to my house, then I guess she also didn't tell you why she was going, right?"

He looked at me with polite disinterest, as if he were reviewing his to-do list while he waited for me to finish chattering.

"She came to see Lev . . . my dad."

His smile didn't waver, but I could tell from the way his eyes sharpened their focus on me that I had gotten to him. I imagined him like one of those clowns in that old song — smiling on the outside, crying on the inside.

"Yeah?" he said. "What did she want with him?"

"She wanted to talk to him. Did you know she was scared, Danny? She was really scared."

Nothing.

I shook my head again. "I don't get you," I said. "I heard you and Tessa were really close. I heard there wasn't a brother and sister on the planet who were closer than you two. I thought you cared about her."

His smile slid off his face. "You don't know anything about my sister and me."

"I know she was scared and she came to my house because she wanted to talk to my father . . . I know — "

Someone grabbed me from behind. It was so unexpected that I pretty much jumped out of my skin. Then someone — presumably the same some-

128

one who had grabbed me — started to laugh.

"Boo!" he said.

I twisted around, trying to break free. I should have guessed. It was Jordan. He was still hanging onto my arm. I shoved him away. Marcus Tyrell was with him. He laughed too.

"You've got a hot little temper, don't you?" he said.

Little temper? I'm surprised he didn't say *cute* little temper. Guys like him make me want to hurl.

"Hey, Danny," Marcus said, "you didn't tell me you had a new girlfriend."

Right. A guy's talking to a girl, therefore she must be his girlfriend. Give the guy an A+ in Neanderthal Logic 101.

"She's just leaving," Danny said.

No, I wasn't, not until I had given it one more try. I said, "Don't you want to know what Te— "

He shoved me. He shoved me so hard I almost fell over.

"I don't want to talk about my sister, okay?" he said. "She's dead. She was my sister and she's dead and I wish everyone would just shut up about her."

Okay, now I was ready to fall over on my own accord. Prince Charming had suddenly turned into a rather nasty Mr. Aggressive.

"Danny — "

"I think he wants you to leave now," Marcus said.

I took a step toward him, but found my way blocked by Jordan.

"The guy just lost his sister," he said. "If he

129

doesn't want to talk about her, he doesn't have to."

There didn't seem to be any point in arguing with him. He didn't want to talk. Fine. Okay. I surrendered. For now.

* * *

I didn't care whether his alibi checked out or not. I didn't care that Mrs. Morgan seemed to trust him with her kids. I didn't even care that her kids seemed to like him. Tom Courtney made me nervous — and suspicious. Maybe it was because he was always standing so close to Mrs. Morgan. When he was with her, there were never more than a few inches between them. I would have been screaming for air if anyone stood that close to me all the time. Or maybe it was the way he kept checking the windows. He couldn't seem to walk past one without glancing out of it, and then, when he did, he gave the whole vista a quick scan, as if he were looking for something. The cops, maybe? If you ask me, it was classic guilty behavior. Most people, unless they're total sociopaths, know when they've done something wrong, and worry, at least a little, about getting caught. Okay, so maybe he wasn't anywhere near East Hastings the night Tessa had died. But I couldn't help wondering if he was married. Or maybe Mrs. Morgan was just one of two or more women he was seeing. Or maybe he was cheating his business partners. I'm not sure what was going on, but I knew there was something. It made me glad when he and Mrs. Morgan finally left for an evening up in Morrisville.

"So, guys," I said to Tyler and Amanda, "what do you want to do tonight? Do you want to watch a movie?" To tell the truth, I was getting tired of movies. "Or how about we do something more fun?" They looked at me expectantly. Uh-oh. I had hinted at "more fun," but I didn't have any idea of what this might be.

"Hide-and-seek!" Tyler shouted. "Let's play hide-and-seek!"

I ran that through the baby-sitter safety filter. On the upside: great potential for not just fun, but for suspense and surprise too. On the downside: little kids can hide in funny — as in strange, not as in hilarious — places. Once when my older sister Brynn and I were a lot younger, we had conned Phoebe into playing hide-and-seek. We had told her that the longer she stayed hidden, the better it meant she was at the game and, if she totally stumped us, we would buy her ice cream. I was It, so I covered my eyes and counted to a hundred. Brynn didn't bother hiding. Phoebe took off. When I finished counting, Brynn was sitting on the couch painting her toenails with Mom's nail polish. I turned on the TV. We didn't start looking for Phoebe until hours later, when we realized that Mom would soon be home. Then, of course, we couldn't find her. We tore the place apart, we begged her to come out, we offered her all kinds of bribes and still no Phoebe. About the tenth time I passed it, I stopped and looked at an old wicker trunk in the storage area behind the kitchen, near where the back stairs were. I thumped on it good and hard and was rewarded by a yelp of surprise from inside.

"Phoebe, you come out right this minute or we won't get you any ice cream after all," I told her.

That's when we both discovered that the trunk was locked. She couldn't get out. She didn't know where the key was. She said she hadn't locked it, which made sense, because she would have had to lock it from the outside. I tried not to panic — it could have been worse, she could have locked herself in an airtight trunk instead of a woven one. But when Phoebe realized we didn't have the key and didn't have a clue where it was, she started to scream. Mom chose that exact moment to get home from work. She wouldn't believe it was an accident — looking back, I can't blame her. Phoebe was a real pain when she was little, and Brynn and I were usually short on patience. Mom also refused to believe that she hadn't warned us about the stupid trunk — there was something wrong with the locking mechanism, so sometimes the trunk locked when you shut it. Sometimes, apparently, it didn't. It took Mom twenty minutes to find the key. By then Phoebe was completely hysterical. She got her ice cream that evening. Brynn and I got grounded.

"We can play hide-and-seek on one condition," I told Tyler and Amanda. "There have to be some ground rules."

First I explained to them what ground rules were. Then I spelled them out. Rule number one, absolutely no hiding in trunks. Rule number two, all hide-and-seek activity had to be confined to the ground floor and second floor of the house. The basement was off limits. So was outside. Rule number three, if they heard me call the magic word — I decided on ice cream — they were to show themselves immediately. They agreed and the game was on.

I had more fun playing hide-and-seek with those two than I ever did with my sisters. Amanda was clever: In one round, she wriggled into a shadowy place in the back of the closet where I couldn't see her and I had to give up. Another time she managed to flatten herself under the billowy eiderdown on her mother's bed so that I had to feel the bed to figure out she was there. Tyler was another story. He never hid himself behind or in anything small enough to conceal him. Once I found him squirreled under a chair in the dining room with his face in his hands so that he couldn't see me. Another time his was one of the faces looking out from the plush faces of the several dozen stuffed animals that were heaped in one corner of Amanda's room. I saw him right away, but pretended I hadn't and went around the room saying, "Where's Tyler? Where can he be? I've looked for him everywhere. Maybe he's . . . under the bed!" I ducked down and looked. "No, he's not there. Maybe he's . . . in the closet!" I grabbed the closet door and wrenched it open. I went around almost the whole room that way, pretending not to see Tyler until he was giggling so hard it was impossible to pretend anymore.

We were about half an hour into the game. I had just found Amanda under the sink in the kitchen and was upstairs looking for Tyler when I heard a knocking sound. At first I thought it was Tyler. Then I heard the door open downstairs. I checked my watch. It was far too early for Mrs. Morgan to be home. Then I heard a scream — a loud, hair-raising scream. As I bounded down the stairs to see what was the matter, I promised myself that I would never again get involved in a game of hide-and-seek.

Chapter 11

I found Amanda in the foyer. The front door was wide-open and a man was standing on the stoop outside. It was Andrew Morgan, Tyler and Amanda's father.

"Daddy!" Amanda cried, and she shrieked again. She threw herself into his arms. "Daddy, we thought you had gone away!" He caught her and twirled her around, hugging her tightly.

"Hi, Pumpkin," he said. "Boy, have I ever missed you." He kissed her and hugged her again before turning to look into the house. "Where's your brother?"

"He's hiding," Amanda said. "We're playing hide-and-seek. You want to come in and play with us, Daddy?"

Not while I was in charge, I thought. I planted myself squarely in the doorway to block him from entering. But he didn't even try to get past me. He held fast to Amanda and whispered something in her ear. She nodded solemnly and whispered something back. Then he set her down and she scampered back inside.

"I think you should leave," I said. I started to close the door, but he put a hand out and stopped me.

"You don't know anything about this," he said.

"All you know is what she tells you, and what she says isn't true."

She — Mrs. Morgan — hadn't told me anything.

"Let go of the door, Mr. Morgan," I said. "If you don't — "

"If I don't, you'll what?" he said. Suddenly he wasn't sweet daddy anymore. He had transformed into Mr. Not-So-Nice-Guy. "What can you possibly do to me that hasn't been done already? Take my kids away? They've been taken. For now. But if you or anyone else thinks that it's going to stay that way, you'd better think again."

He was talking quietly, but his eyes blazed into me. He was giving me the creeps. Keep calm, I told myself. If the guy's some kind of lunatic, the worst thing you can do is let him smell your fear.

"If you don't let me close this door right now, Mr. Morgan, I'll go back inside and call the police," I said. I looked him straight in the eyes when I said it, and as I did, I made myself repeat over and over to myself, I am not afraid, I am not afraid.

Finally his hand fell away from the door.

"They're my kids," he said, "and anyone who thinks they can keep them from me is sadly mistaken."

He turned and started down the steps. I slammed the door before his foot hit the second step and bolted it long before he was all the way down. I walked straight into the kitchen and reached for the telephone. My hands were trembling as I started dialing my home phone number.

I hung up again before I finished, though. Mr. Morgan was right, I didn't know the whole story. The person I needed to talk to was Mrs. Morgan.

I found the kids together in Amanda's room.

"Is Daddy gone?" she said.

I said he was. Then I said, "I guess it's been a while since you've seen him, huh?"

She nodded. "Mommy said he had to go away."

"Oh?" Keep it light, Chloe. Don't act strange and maybe they won't act strange. "Where did he go?"

"Just away," Amanda said. "Mommy said she didn't know when he was coming back or where he was. She just said he had to go."

"Well, you looked like you were pretty happy to see him," I said. Then, still trying to keep it casual, "What did he whisper to you?"

Bad move. She shook her head and I had no trouble reading the mistrust in her eyes.

"It's a secret," she said.

I didn't push it. But when Mrs. Morgan came home, I told her what had happened.

Her face went pale. "He was here? My husband was here?" She glanced at Tom Courtney, who immediately went to the window and peered out into the darkness. "Are you sure it was my husband?"

"Amanda called him Daddy."

She looked again at Tom Courtney. He turned away from the window and shook his head.

"If something's wrong, you could call the police," I said.

"No," she said, just like that, without even think-

137

ing about it. "No police. This is nobody's business but my own."

"But if you're scared — "

"How much do I owe you?" she said. She started rummaging in her purse for some money, and thrust a couple of bills into my hand. It was too much, but when I tried to say so, she said, "Tom will drive you home." This time I didn't protest.

Tom Courtney wasn't the talkative type. He asked me where I lived. I told him and asked if he needed directions. He nodded, so I told him exactly how to get from the Morgans' house to mine. We drove the whole way in silence. Then, when he pulled into my driveway, he said, "I hope you'll respect Mrs. Morgan's wishes."

I said I would. I'm not sure I would have kept my word if Levesque had been home, but he wasn't. He and Mom had gone out for the evening, and they weren't back yet. By the next morning, I had made two decisions. One, I wasn't going to mess around in anyone's business if they didn't want me to. And, two, the next time Mrs. Morgan called me to baby-sit, if she ever called me again, I was going to say no, and it didn't matter who heard me say it, I was going to stand my ground.

* * *

By noon the next day I had a headache. It was one of those stayed-up-too-late-studying-for-a-math-test headaches. At least the test was over. The plus side of staying up so late was that I was pretty sure I had done well. But that didn't make the throbbing go away, so I went outside, despite the fact that winter had returned with a vengeance during the night and had dumped a full six inches of snow on East Hastings. It was snowing again when I went out, big, flat, fluffy flakes that stuck to my hair and my coat, the kind of snow that looks great on Christmas Eve when you're watching old movies on TV while you wrap those last few gifts, but that doesn't seem so great when you're thinking about driveways and front walks and the fact that — come on, already! — isn't spring just around the corner?

But even that didn't stop me from sauntering out into the schoolyard and sucking in a few lungfuls of cold, crisp, snowy air. Just the thing for a headache.

The dull ache was easing a little when I noticed Jake leaning against one of the emergency exit doors, his head turned away from me. I thought maybe he hadn't noticed me, so I headed over to him. I felt bad about what Ross had done and, to be honest, I was afraid Jake thought I'd had something to do with it. But just as I drew close, he stepped away from the door and strode away. That's when it hit me. He had seen me and had turned away to avoid me. He probably held me at least partly to blame for Ross's actions. If there's one thing I hate, it's people thinking things about me that just aren't true.

"Hey, Jake!" I called. I ran after him.

He kept walking. I had to move faster and kind

of dance around in front of him to make him look at me.

"Hey, what's the matter?" I asked.

He scowled at me. His right hand was wrapped in an elastic bandage, the result of his having slammed it into the locker room wall.

"What's the matter?" he echoed.

"That was the question. Look, I know you're mad at Ross, and I know he's my friend, but — "

"You told him, didn't you?" he said. Bingo. I was right. He had me cast as a villain. "What I said to you was just between you and me. I told you about that night because I wanted you to give a message to your dad, that's all. I didn't tell you so that you could blab it to Jenkins and it would end up all over the school."

"I didn't tell Ross anything," I said.

"Then how did he find out?"

"You tell me." I did my best to look honest and trustworthy. "Maybe that friend of yours who told the police he called you the night Tessa died, also happened to mention the same thing to someone else. Maybe he happened to mention a few other things besides," I said. "But I didn't do it. That's not the way I operate. I'm completely innocent."

His lip curled a little.

"Me, too," he said. "That's the point. I'm completely innocent and I'm sick of people acting like I'm not. I didn't hurt her."

From the trembling passion in his voice to the burning intensity of his eyes, he seemed exactly what he claimed to be — a guy who was deeply hurt by the idea that seemed to be circulating that he might not only have hurt, but might actually have killed, his girlfriend. He peered at me and then, as a bell rang somewhere behind us, he strode away across the snowy field, leaving a track behind him that was quickly filled in by the silent falling snow.

* * *

I was in history class where I was supposed to be concentrating on the rebellion of 1837 and what would make perfectly nice middle-class people in what was then Upper Canada rise up against the prevailing social order. What I was actually concentrating on was Jake Bailey — how he seemed so sincere about his innocence, but how he had behaved when he had told me about that night, how he had seemed to be clutching at anything that would explain why he might not have heard the phone when it rang. And I was thinking about the two guys, Howie Moss and Dave LeMatt, who had led Jake Bailey out of the jeering circle the day that Jake had been ready to kick the . . . Well, let's just say, to teach Ross a lesson. Doing what they had done that day showed that they cared about Jake and didn't want him to get in any trouble. That must mean they were Jake's friends.

Then I thought about what Jake had said, that one of his friends had told the police that he hadn't answered the phone the night Tessa was murdered. I wondered if that friend had been Howie or

Dave. I decided that now might be a good time to find out. Trouble was, I didn't really know either of them and had no idea where they lived. Which meant that I had to run all the way from the third floor — French class, my last class of the day — down to the front door of the school, and more or less stake it out, scanning every face. I knew perfectly well that there were nearly a dozen exits from the school and that either Howie or Dave could be using any one of those even as I was glued to the foyer.

Then the rush finished. The foyer was almost empty and my hope of spotting either of them had melted away like snowflakes tracked inside. I buttoned my coat, heaved my backpack onto my back and groaned under the weight of half a dozen hard, unyielding textbooks. I pulled on my mittens and hat, headed outside — and almost collided with Dave LeMatt.

"Hi," I said.

He peered at me as if he were trying to place me. I could tell by his baffled look that he wasn't having any success.

"You're a friend of Jake's, right?" I said.

He nodded slowly and looked a lot like a guy who had stumbled into a fortuneteller's tent and was genuinely astonished when she told him his age or what he was preoccupied with — sports or girls — when, come on, what seventeen-year-old guy wasn't preoccupied with those two things?

"Jake tells me you called him that night," I said.

The fortuneteller had misspoken. The spell was broken. Dave's look was one of pure disdain.

"That wasn't me," he said. "That was Howie. And let me tell you something, even if it had been me who had called Jake that night, I would never have ratted him out to the police. I'm not that kind of guy."

Right. He was the other kind of guy. The kind who was inclined to obstruct justice. A good friend and all-around upstanding citizen.

Howie Moss had made the phone call and Howie Moss had told the police about it, according to Dave LeMatt.

"You know where I could find Howie?"

Dave looked hard at me.

"Why?"

"Because I want to talk to him."

"About what?"

When I had seen Dave out on the field, when I had watched him go up to Jake and touch his shoulder and then lead him out of that howling circle and off the field, I had thought he must be a pretty nice guy, a guy who really cared about his friend, the kind of guy I might even want to get to know. He seemed to have that sweet, sensitive thing going for him. It definitely wasn't going for him now. He was probably still being a friend to Jake. He didn't want Jake to get into any trouble. But he wasn't being helpful to me and it didn't look like that was going to change any time soon.

"Never mind," I said.

He shrugged, turned and walked away.

I didn't know Howie Moss. I didn't know where he hung out, what his hobbies were, or what he liked to do when he wasn't in school. I didn't even know whether or not he liked school. Because I didn't know anything about Howie. I had no idea where to look for him. So I turned turn to the handiest people-locator I know, the telephone book.

There were two Mosses listed in the East Hastings phone book. They both lived on the same street. In fact, judging from the street numbers listed in the phone book, they lived right next to each other. Two generations would have been my guess. In any case, it sure was convenient.

One of the Moss houses was a large, sturdy stone building that once had sat alone on a wide in-town lot. I say once because now, nestled so close to it that it was like a baby cradled in the crook of its mother's arm, was a much smaller, perfectly square bungalow. Grandma's house, I thought. Or maybe Grandpa's. I headed for the larger of the two houses and rang the bell. Howie answered. He gave me a look vacuum cleaner salesmen were probably used to, but I wasn't.

"I'm Chloe," I said. "I go to your school?" I don't know why, maybe it was the hard look he was giving me, but what was supposed to be a statement came out as a question, as if I were asking him to confirm my enrollment at East Hastings Regional.

"Yeah," he said. "So?"

"So, I'm a friend of Jake's."

His eyes narrowed. "Since when?" he said. So far

as I knew, I had given him no reason to put that nasty edge in his voice, but it was there all the same.

"Since some of his other friends started wondering if he had anything to do with what happened to Tessa."

He just stared at me.

"Jake thinks you ratted him out to the police," I said.

That got a reaction.

"I didn't rat out anyone! Besides, what was I supposed to do? The cops were asking questions."

"How come they asked you about Jake?"

He shrugged. His eyes avoided mine. "All I know is, I was in class and I got called down to the office and the cops were there and wanted to ask me what I knew about Jake and about the night Tessa died."

Levesque or Steve Denby must have gone to the school and asked who Jake's friends were.

"They asked me, had I seen Jake that night. I said no. Then — " His eyes shifted away from me. "Then I guess I told them that I had called him that night, but that no one had answered the phone."

"You just volunteered that information?" I asked.

His head drooped a little. "It wasn't like I meant to say it. It just kind of popped out."

"Just kind of popped out?" Maybe it was true, but I wasn't buying it. If Levesque had asked me where Ross was that night and I had tried calling him

145

and he wasn't there, I don't think I would have necessarily told him — geez, Levesque would have been blazing if he knew what I was thinking — but I don't think I would have volunteered that information without at least talking to Ross first. Not unless I thought something was seriously wrong. Not unless I had some reason to.

"You've known Jake for a while, haven't you?"

"Ever since he moved here."

"Do you think he did it?"

His head came up slowly, but once his eyes met mine, they didn't waver.

"I don't know," he said. "That's what I told the cops. I know Jake and Tessa were having problems. And I know Jake went nuts when she started hanging around with Jenkins. And . . . " His voice dropped off.

"And what?" I prodded.

"Nothing," he said.

"And he had a pretty bad temper, right?" No response. "Did you ever see him hurt Tessa?" No answer. This particular all-news station seemed to have signed off for the day. But I would have bet every dollar I had that Levesque had asked the same question. And I would have bet that he had gotten an answer.

"Jake says he was at home," I said quietly.

"If he was at home, why didn't he pick up the phone?"

That, of course, was the million-dollar question.

Chapter 12

I was walking home from Howie Moss's house when I saw Andrew Morgan. He appeared suddenly on the side of the road in front of the abandoned gas station that stood all alone, around a bend just half a mile past where the stores and the banks on Centre Street sort of petered out. From the gas station, you have a pretty good view of a field on one side of the road and another field on the other. In other words, there's nothing around.

He seemed to pop out of nowhere, as if a magician had pulled him out of a hat, which meant that by the time I saw him, I didn't have much chance to cross the street to avoid him. Then, just as I started to scramble to steer clear of him, the closest of the three stoplights on Centre Street changed from red to green and along came, well, not exactly a steady stream of traffic, but enough cars and trucks that I couldn't get across the road before Andrew Morgan got to me. He was smiling when he reached me.

"Did you have a chance to think over my request?" he said.

Vehicular traffic in East Hastings is a little like cops everywhere else — there's never any when you need some. By now the trucks and cars had gone past and there I was, alone on a relatively secluded stretch of road with this man. I decided to play dumb.

"What request?" I said.

"You said you'd consider helping me get custody of my kids."

Funny, I didn't remember ever saying that. And even if I had said it, I would have retracted it after the way he had acted when he showed up at the house.

"Look, Mr. Morgan, I don't really think this is any of my business." As I spoke, I was trying to edge around him. He would have made a good goalie. He blocked me at every turn.

"I'll pay you," he said, and pulled some money from his pocket. Twenties. Three or four of them. "All I want to know is, what does she do with her spare time? Is she seeing anyone? Who is she seeing?"

What did that have to do with custody of Tyler and Amanda? I wondered.

"Maybe what you need is a lawyer," I suggested, and made another stab at getting past him. He stopped me by grabbing one of my arms. Foul. That's when I said something absolutely brilliant. I said, "Let go of me."

His response was to tighten his grip. He started to drag me away from the side of the road.

"What is it with you?" he said. "Are all you females hard-wired to stick together? Solidarity forever, is that it?" His fingers were biting into my arm, even though I was wearing a sweater and a jacket. "All I want is a little information. Is that so much to ask?"

"Let go of me, Mr. Morgan," I said. I don't know if he noticed that my voice was trembling, but it was, and I sure noticed. "If you don't let go, I'm going to start screaming and keep on screaming until you leave me alone."

Maybe that would have been enough to make him let go, maybe not. But suddenly I got lucky. I heard a car behind me and I twisted around and with my free hand, I waved at it. Maybe that made him think I knew the driver or maybe it just scared him, but he let go. The minute he did, I ran toward the car, waving both arms now and shouting for it to stop. In the city, that would have been a signal for the driver to hit the gas and get out of there as fast as possible. But this wasn't the city, it was East Hastings. The driver hit the brakes. That was enough to make Mr. Morgan back off. He scurried away around the side of the abandoned gas station. The driver of the car, who turned out to be a woman who worked at the Canadian Tire with my mother, leaned across to the passenger-side window. Lucille Travers cranked the window down and called out to me, "Everything okay, Chloe?"

I nodded. Then I saw a car come around the side of the abandoned gas station. It was silver-gray. I was pretty sure it was the same silver-gray car that I had seen out on our street the afternoon Tessa had come looking for Levesque. I peered at it, trying to catch the license number. AE—

A car door slammed and someone touched my shoulder, startling me into looking away from Andrew Morgan's car.

"Chloe?" Lucille said.

By the time I looked back at the car, it had vanished.

"Are you okay?" Lucille said. She was peering intently at me. "Was that man bothering you?"

I shook my head.

"Ever since poor Tessa," she said, and left the verb unspoken. "Well, I guess you can't be too careful, right? Can I give you a lift home?"

Originally I had been heading home, but now I decided on a change of course. I shook my head.

"You sure I can't give you a ride somewhere?"

That's when I noticed that my legs were trembling. No doubt about it, Andrew Morgan had scared me. When he had me by the arm, even though it wasn't yet dark, I had thought, so this is how Tessa must have felt. Except that where she was, there had been no chance of a car going by. And even if she had started shouting, even if she had screamed, there would have been nobody around to hear her. His fingers would have bitten into her arms and maybe she had fought back. But there had been no passerby to scare him off. I had been lucky.

I looked at Lucille and was sure I was looking at my own personal guardian angel. "Do you think you could drive me to the police station?" I said.

She nodded and opened the passenger-side door

for me. When we got to the station, she pulled over and got out and opened the door for me. "Do you want me to come inside with you?" she asked.

"No, I'm fine." Then a thought occurred to me. "Lucille?"

She looked expectantly at me.

"Don't tell my mom about this, okay?"

She nodded.

Levesque was standing beside what looked like a first-generation filing cabinet when I opened the door to the station house. A battered coffee maker sat on top of it and he was pouring himself a cup of coffee. He turned when he heard the door. At first he didn't look exactly delighted to see me. But after he had scrutinized me, something in his eyes changed. He set down his cup and came toward me.

"What's wrong?" he said.

It was as if he had punched a hole in my retaining wall. All of a sudden I was spilling out words. He sat me down on a hard wooden chair and then pulled up another one and sat opposite me. He let me talk and talk until I had babbled out the whole convoluted story — Andrew Morgan, what he had wanted, the silver car, Tessa baby-sitting for the Morgans. When I had finished, he got up and got me a glass of water. After I had drunk it, he said, "Okay. So you say the first time this Andrew Morgan approached you was in the park?" Then he took me through the whole thing all over, in order this time, asking me question after question until he had sorted out the entire sequence of events.

When he seemed to have it all settled in his mind, he got up and grabbed his coat from a hook in the back room.

"Come on," he said. "I'm taking you home."

My mother opened the front door before the car even came to a stop in our driveway. I hoped Lucille Travers never had to take an oath of silence. She wouldn't last two minutes. I don't think she had even lasted one.

"Are you okay?" my mother asked anxiously. Phoebe was standing behind her, peering out at me.

"I'm fine," I said. But if that was so, why was I trembling all over? And why, even though it was now about an hour since he had grabbed me, could I still feel his fingers biting into me?

"Give her something to eat and something warm to drink," Levesque said. "She'll be okay." He laid a hand on my shoulder. "Right?"

I nodded. While my mother shepherded me inside, Levesque went back down the steps and got back into his car. I guessed he was going back to work. I guessed he was going to try to find Andrew Morgan.

My mother pulled off my jacket. She hadn't done that since I was maybe four or five years old. She pressed one warm hand flat against one of my cheeks.

"You're cold," she said. My teeth were chattering, even though it was nice and warm inside the house and I could hear the furnace rumbling. "Why don't you go upstairs and get into bed? I'll make you some soup."

She didn't need to tell me twice. I went upstairs and climbed under the quilt on my bed. Almost as soon as I did, Shendor showed up and shoved her face at me. I scratched her behind the ears. Her tail wagged happily, then she positioned herself across the bottom of my bed. I pulled my quilt up around my neck. Someone knocked on my door.

"Yeah?" I said.

It wasn't Mom with soup. It was Phoebe. Her eyes were wide as she crept in. Generally speaking, she wasn't welcome in my room. It wasn't that I didn't like my kid sister. It's just that, well, she *was* my kid sister.

"Are you okay?" she asked.

I don't know what it was — the hushed way she spoke, like she was entering a sickroom; the way she was looking at me, like she was expecting to see a ghost and seemed relieved that I hadn't turned out to be one; or just the fact that my little sister was here at all, looking relieved that I was safe and sound. Whichever it was, suddenly tears were burning my eyes and before I could turn away, Phoebe had snagged a few tissues from the box on my dresser and was pressing them into my hand.

"He didn't hurt you, did he?" she asked.

I shook my head while I snuffled into the wad of tissue, then blotted at my eyes. I hate crying, especially when there's nothing to cry about. I was fine. He hadn't hurt me. Okay, so the creep had scared me a little, and he had made me think what a jerk I was to Tessa when she was probably just as scared as I had been. If only I had asked her why she wanted to talk to Levesque. But he hadn't hurt me.

"Dad's going to get him," Phoebe said. "It's going to be okay."

I had no quarrel with the first part of what she said. I wasn't so sure about the second part. Then there was my mother, with a bowl of something steaming and a mug of something else steaming, both carried on a tray.

"Cream of mushroom soup," she said. My favorite. "And some apple cinnamon tea."

While I sat up, Phoebe grabbed the lap desk that was propped up against the side of my bed and handed it to me. Mom set down the tray and Phoebe started to back toward the door.

"Actually, Pheebs," I said, "I wouldn't mind a little company." I hadn't said that too often before, but, boy, I had never meant it more than I did at that moment.

"Really?" she said.

I nodded. "How about I show you again what a genius I am at cribbage?"

The soup was fine. So was the tea. Together, they shook away the tremors. The cribbage was a bust — for me. Phoebe skunked me twice, gleefully. While she did, I wondered exactly when she had grown so confident, when she had gotten so good at *my* game, and, to tell the truth, how I could have managed to live for so long in the same house as someone who, lately, was constantly surprising me.

My plan was to wait up for Levesque to come

home and then to grill him for information. I figured I wouldn't have a problem because I figured I wasn't going to get much sleep. Every time I closed my eyes, I felt Andrew Morgan's fingers digging into my arms. I was going to stay awake because I couldn't sleep, and when I heard Levesque come in, I was going to find out what he had found out. Just let him try to tell me to keep my nose out of police business when I was the one who had brought him that business. But the best laid plans, right? The next thing I knew, my mother was shaking me awake. "You're going to be late for school," she said, "and I have to get to work."

I rolled out of bed. By the time I had my robe on, I heard the front door close. I ran down to the front door and saw my mother's car pulling out of the driveway. Levesque's car was nowhere in sight.

"Was he here this morning?" I asked Phoebe, who was in the kitchen, chowing down on cold cereal.

"Who?" she said.

"There's you, me, Mom, and Shendor," I said. "All female. Then there's Levesque."

"You mean, Dad?"

He wasn't my dad. I liked him, but he wasn't my dad, he wasn't Phoebe's dad, and he wasn't Brynn's dad.

"Was he here this morning?" I asked again.

She shook her head. "Not when I got up."

* * *

We had lived in East Hastings for nine months, so, really, I shouldn't have been surprised at the speed at which news traveled in town. Ross rang the doorbell before I had even gathered my books and shoved them into my backpack.

"You think it was him?" he said, when I opened the door. I had to fight the urge to say, "Really, I'm fine, thanks for asking."

"You think it was him what?" I said.

"Andrew Morgan. You think he was the one who . . . hurt Tessa?"

"What are you talking about, Ross?"

"He threatened you, didn't he? That's what I heard. He threatened you because you wouldn't help him get some information about Mrs. Morgan. He could have threatened Tessa too. He could have done more than threaten her."

I guess that meant he had let go of his pitbull grip on Jake Bailey as the guilty party.

"I don't know, Ross," I said. I had slept all night. At least, I didn't remember anything about last night, so I assumed I had slept through it. But I still felt tired. Not tired as in yawning all the time, but tired as in sort of headachy and dragged down, as if I had run a marathon in my sleep. "We should get going or we're going to be late for school," I said.

Ross looked disappointed. No juicy details were being served out at my table this morning. We trudged in silence down my street, along to town and up Centre Street toward school. We were about half a block from the police station when a patrol car pulled up.

"Come on," Ross said. "Let's go ask him." What

he really meant was, come on, Chloe, *you* ask him.
I grabbed Ross's arm to hold him back.

The driver's-side and the passenger-side doors
opened at almost exactly the same time. Steve
Denby got out of the driver's side. Levesque unfold-
ed himself from the passenger-side seat. He
reached for the rear passenger-side door and
opened it. One of his hands reached in and he
pulled — yanked — a man from the back seat. It
was Andrew Morgan. His hands were cuffed
behind his back. Levesque pushed his head down
so that he didn't clunk it against the doorframe,
but he shoved him forward at the same time so
that Andrew Morgan stumbled when his foot hit
the pavement. If Levesque hadn't had a firm grip
— it looked like an iron grip — on Morgan's collar,
he might have fallen. Levesque's face was grim.
More than that, he looked angry. Furious, really,
and I tried to remember when I had seen that
expression on his face before. I pulled a blank. I
tried to tell myself that Andrew Morgan deserved
any treatment he got, and maybe that would have
been true if he had been arrested by someone else.
But this was Levesque. He was a good guy, and
good guys weren't supposed to use bad-guy tactics.
They weren't supposed to shove and bully. They
weren't supposed to push around some guy who
couldn't fight back. They were supposed to take the
high road. Yet here was Levesque, literally head
and shoulders taller than Andrew Morgan, pulling
and then prodding forward a guy who was already

handcuffed and helpless. I didn't want to be seeing this. I didn't want to think of him the way some people think of cops, like thugs with guns, badges and a lot of power who sometimes let that go to their heads. I hurried into the first open door, which happened to be the drugstore, and I stood there for a long time in front of a display of chewing gum, pretending that I was trying to decide which kind I wanted to buy when, really, I wasn't even seeing gum, I was seeing Levesque angrily shoving Andrew Morgan ahead of him into the police station.

"Hey," said a voice beside me. Ross's voice. "What gives?"

I reached out and picked a pack of spearmint. Then I dug in my pocket for enough nickels and dimes and quarters to pay for it. I took my time. I wanted to make sure that when we went back out into the street, Levesque would be gone.

"You okay?" Ross asked.

I nodded. But I wasn't so sure.

Chapter 13

I went to homeroom. I went to math class. I don't remember anything about the class, but I know I was there because Ms. Pileggi called on me to answer a question and the best I could do was stare blankly at her because, to tell the truth, I hadn't heard the question. She didn't yell at me, though, and she didn't give me extra work, which is what she usually does when she catches people wool-gathering, as she calls it, in class. What is that supposed to mean, anyway? Wool-gathering? Anyway, I guessed she must be on the Lucille Travers grapevine because she just looked at me, not even in an annoyed way, and sighed and asked someone else a question. It may even have been the same question.

After math class, I was supposed to go to French. I didn't, though. I walked down to the very end of the hall and let myself out an exit door, then I walked clear across the schoolyard and wriggled through the gap in the chain link fence that separated the school from a meadow that ran down to a stream. The edges of it were frozen, but the water still bubbled along in the middle and I thought I'd sit there and listen to it. I like the sound of running water. I like the way it looks, too, running along, always going someplace, always coming from someplace else. It was cold out, I could see my breath, so I figured I'd be alone. I was wrong.

Jake Bailey had claimed a rock by the edge of the stream. He was squatting on a boulder and was tearing up a piece of paper and scattering the confetti-sized pieces into the middle of the stream so that they were carried along, up and down, under the water and then on top of it, going someplace, someplace else. When I saw Jake, I started to turn away. But, "Hey," he called to me. "Hey, what's the matter with everyone?"

Everyone? Was he seeing me in triplicate?

"Am I invisible all of a sudden?"

I turned to look at him. What was he talking about?

"Oh, so you see me after all," he said. "Because I was beginning to wonder what would happen if I looked into a mirror. Would it be a vampire-type thing, would I not see my own reflection?"

"Look, Jake — "

"Yup," he said, nodding, "you see me all right. What does that mean? Do you have special powers, or am I still among the living?"

"What's your problem?"

"My problem?" He scattered the last bits of paper into the water. Some of it missed, though, and fell onto the ice and stuck there. "My problem is that people think I hurt Tessa."

He thought he had problems. I looked down at the tiny bits of paper and wondered what he had been shredding. I wondered, too, where the word hurt had come from. Ross had said the same thing this morning. Did I think that Andrew Morgan was the one who had hurt Tessa? Hurt? Come on, guys, someone had done more than hurt Tessa. She was dead. Dead and buried.

"It doesn't matter, Jake," I said. And it didn't. Not now, not with Andrew Morgan and his rage and his silver-gray car. I wondered if Jake had heard about that, and thought maybe he hadn't. The news seemed to have traveled purely by word of mouth and with so few people talking to Jake these days, the grapevine probably didn't include him.

"It matters to me," Jake said. "It matters that people think I did something I didn't do."

"They don't — "

"They do. Even my friends do. And then your friend ran that article in the school paper, and now everyone thinks I'm some kind of thug who can't be trusted, who maybe even hurt his girlfriend. I didn't do anything."

"Except lie," I muttered. Maybe I meant for him to hear me, maybe I didn't. He heard, though.

"What's that supposed to mean?" he asked, all self-righteous.

"I talked to Howie Moss," I said. "He was the one who called you that night. You didn't answer the phone. Where were you, Jake?"

"I told you — "

"You lied to me." At least, I was pretty sure he had lied, because someone sure wasn't telling the truth, and it was either Jake or Howie, and why would Howie lie about having called Jake? "You

161

lied to me and you lied to the cops. You weren't home when you said you were. And I'm supposed to feel sorry for you because people don't believe you? Give me a break."

He stared at me for a moment, his body rigid, as if he were poised to pounce on me and shove me into the stream, or poised to jump into the stream and try to drown himself. Poised, in other words, to do something drastic.

"I wasn't with Tessa that night," he said.

"Fine," I said. "Whatever. No reason why you should tell me anything. You say you weren't with her. Howie says you weren't home. Maybe you think the cops are stupid, but they're not. These things can be checked, Jake. They've probably been checked already." I turned away from him. Suddenly the stream was one more place I didn't want to be.

When he grabbed me, I reacted. Some people would even say I overreacted. I felt his hand on my arm and I thought of Andrew Morgan and how his fingers had dug into me. I whirled around and grabbed at him and shoved him away from me as hard as I could. I guess he wasn't expecting that because a look of surprise jumped onto his face and then, all of a sudden, he was falling away from me, his arms pinwheeling in the air, scrabbling for a handhold . . . only there was no handhold to be had. I grabbed the front of his jacket before he lost his footing completely and fell back into the stream.

"Don't touch me," I said, as I struggled to keep him upright.

"Don't walk away from me when I'm talking to you," he snarled, which took a lot of nerve because he said it while his footing was still precarious and while it would have been oh-so-easy for me to let go and even give him another little shove backwards. But I didn't. I helped him regain the balance I had caused him to lose and once I was sure he wasn't going to topple, I turned away from him again. This time he didn't grab me. This time he circled around me.

"Okay," he said, "so I wasn't home that night. Is that a crime?"

I could have told him about Andrew Morgan. I could have let him know that he was already off the hook. Maybe I would have if he hadn't acted like such a jerk and if he hadn't grabbed me.

"It depends where you were and what you were doing," I said.

"I wasn't hurting Tessa."

What was that in his eyes? A sort of looking at me and not looking at me. Trying to make me believe him, but holding something back at the same time, so that if I didn't know what I did about Andrew Morgan, I would have shoved Jake right back to the top of the suspect list and kept him there until I had nailed down every word of what he was saying with at least three independent sources per claim.

"I could save everyone a lot of time," I said. "I could walk down to the cop shop right now and tell them that you just told me you weren't home, that you lied to them before."

There was no mistaking the look in his eyes now. It was out-and-out panic. Flat-out, guilty panic, worse even than I had seen in Ross's eyes when he had admitted he had seen Tessa that night.

"Unless," I said, "you want to tell me exactly what you were doing that night."

He ducked his head for a moment. When he raised it again, he said, "She told me she couldn't see me, but she wouldn't tell me why. I figured it was him."

"Him?"

"Your buddy. Jenkins."

I waited.

He sighed. His shoulders sagged a little. "Okay," he said, and he didn't need to wave a white flag for me to understand that he was surrendering. "Okay, look . . . " His eyes met mine. No evasiveness. No looking away. Just a steady look while he said, "She told me that she wasn't interested in him — "

"In Ross, you mean?"

He nodded. "But she wouldn't tell me why she couldn't see me that night. What was I supposed to think?"

Apparently it would have been too much for him to think that maybe Tessa preferred to keep a few corners of her life private, for herself alone. "So you followed her."

He nodded.

I remembered back when Ross had told me how

nervous Tessa had been that night. She had thought she was being followed. The way it sounded now, she had been leading a parade.

"I saw them together. They were having some kind of argument."

"Which is why you think he hurt her?"

Jake nodded.

"You didn't see what happened after they argued?"

"They argued and then Tessa set off in one direction and Jenkins just stood there for a few minutes, watching her. I figured Tessa was on her way home. I could see that what she had told me was true. It was pretty obvious she wasn't interested in Jenkins. But he still seemed interested in her. He started to follow her again. Then he stopped. Then he started again. I hung around for a while to see what he was going to do. Eventually he headed off in the opposite direction from Tessa, so I figured that was that. But for all I know, he changed his mind again after I left him and he followed her after all. Followed her and got into another argument with her and then — "

And then hurt her, apparently. "Why didn't you just tell the cops the truth?" I asked.

"And make myself the prime suspect?" He shook his head. "There are plenty of people who want to believe I did it. But I didn't. And if my parents thought I was in trouble again . . . " His voice trailed off. "Besides," he said, "I didn't do anything wrong."

Finally Jake had come clean with me. He sounded pretty convincing, too. I figured now was a good time to connect him to the grapevine.

"Jake, did Tessa ever mention a man named Andrew Morgan?"

He frowned. "I don't think so. Why?"

I told him what I knew. I told him he probably didn't have anything to worry about. I wasn't kidding. At the time, that was exactly what I thought.

* * *

I stood on the opposite side of the street from the police station for maybe ten minutes before I decided that maybe I wouldn't go in after all. When I finally crossed the street and pushed the door open, I couldn't decide whether I was relieved or disappointed that Levesque wasn't there.

"Hey, Chloe," Steve Denby said. He smiled at me in his gosh-darned, small-town, friendly cop way. He was a lot younger than Levesque. I think he had been a police officer for a grand total of two and a half years, all of them in East Hastings. He hadn't begun to get jaded the way city cops do. I mean, how grim a view of human nature can you have when you spend most of your time rescuing tourists from the woods and issuing parking tickets? Despite a couple of murders in the past year, East Hastings isn't exactly a high-crime district, and the crimes that are committed are generally committed by regular citizens, not hardened criminals, gang members or drug addicts. So when Steve smiled and said hi, I smiled and said hi right back. Then he said, "If you're looking for the boss, he isn't here."

There was no mistaking it now. I *was* relieved.

"What about Andrew Morgan?" I asked.

"We're still holding him," he said. "We're hoping we can get him in front of a judge pretty soon." That meant that charges had been laid against Morgan, and from the way Steve winked at me, I could tell that he wasn't hoping to see the judge too soon. It seemed that the East Hastings Police Department wanted to keep Andrew Morgan locked up and sweating for as long as it could before allowing a judge to consider the possibility of bail.

"How about you?" Steve asked. "You okay?"

I nodded, but I didn't feel okay. What I felt was Andrew Morgan's fingers biting into my arms as he pulled at me, dragging me away from the road. What if Lucille hadn't come along when she did? Would someone have found *me* face down and dead somewhere?

"See you around, Steve," I said.

* * *

Mrs. Morgan's house does not lie anywhere between the police station and my house, so I can't really explain how I happened to find myself walking past it. But I did and what I saw there surprised me. A big truck sat in the driveway, one of those trucks people rent when they're moving themselves from one place to another. A couple of loading planks ran from the back of the truck to the pavement of the drive, and five or six men were carrying furniture and boxes out of the house and loading them into the truck. One of those men was Levesque. I started to turn away before he could see me, but then someone yelled, "Chloe!" It was Amanda. She came shooting down the driveway toward me. Mrs. Morgan saw her bolt and called her name. That did it. Everyone in the driveway turned to stare at me just as Amanda threw herself into my arms.

"We're going away!" she said, sounding all excited. "We're going someplace really special."

Mrs. Morgan reached us just then. She sent Amanda back to the house and then she said to me, "I hope he didn't hurt you."

I shook my head.

"I'm sorry," she said. "If I had known . . . "

If she had known what? Then Tom Courtney and Levesque were there, standing behind her, and Tom Courtney said, "We're just about ready."

"Where are you going?" I asked.

She didn't answer. Instead, she looked at Levesque, who just said, "You'd better get moving."

I glanced back at the truck. The men who had been loading it were now closing it up and padlocking it shut. I recognized at least one of them from the people in the woods after Tessa had been killed. He was a cop.

Then I saw Tom Courtney climb into the truck, while Mrs. Morgan and the kids got into a car. The car followed the truck down the road and finally disappeared from sight.

"What's going on?" I asked Levesque.

"She's making a fresh start."

"Where?"

He didn't answer.

"What's going on?" I asked again, only now I was mad. What *was* going on?

"It took a lot of courage for her to leave him in the first place," Levesque said. "He used to beat her up."

Oh.

"She thought when she came here, he wouldn't find her. She even changed her name."

I remembered back to the time Tyler had called Amanda, Samantha. She hadn't just changed her name, she had changed the kids' names, too. Which meant that she must have been terrified of Andrew Morgan. I realized then that that wasn't *his* real name, either.

"How did he find her?" I asked.

Levesque shook his head. "Guys like him never give up. That's what makes them so scary. Maybe this time she'll get lucky."

I wasn't sure I understood. "Why does she have to leave?" I asked. "If he killed Tessa, he'll go to prison for a long time."

Usually Levesque was stone-faced. Sometimes he wasn't, but that was only when he wasn't trying to keep you from finding out something. At that exact moment, he couldn't have been easier to read if he were one of those cardboard-paged baby books.

"You don't think he killed Tessa, do you?" I said.

"I'm one hundred percent positive he didn't." He sounded almost as disappointed as I felt. "He's got what appears to be an airtight alibi."

"But he *was* harassing her, wasn't he?"

"He says he asked her a few questions. I think maybe he asked her the same way he asked you. But there's no way he could have killed her. He wasn't anywhere near East Hastings the night it happened."

"Maybe his alibi is lying."

"He was in lock-up over in Sudbury. He gave a waitress five stitches and a very black eye."

"Nice guy," I muttered. "So how come you're still holding him?"

The distaste was obvious on Levesque's face. "Because he *is* such a nice guy. Because he assaulted you. Because he ignored the restraining order that prevents him from being within five hundred yards of Mrs. Morgan or the kids. Because he threatened to kill Mrs. Morgan. Oh yeah, and because he's on parole from beating her up so badly a year ago that he almost killed her, and he broke the conditions of that parole. Frankly, I'm hoping to send him back to prison for the balance of his sentence. It's only another six months, but that will give her a chance to get herself settled someplace else."

I guessed that was something. "What about Tessa?" I said.

He gave me that look. The Official Police Business look.

Chapter 14

Ross was humming with energy, like one of those high-tension, electrical wires that are strung across fields and along highways on the shoulders of giant metal skeletons.

"I knew it," he said. "I knew it was Jake!"

"Yesterday you thought it was Andrew Morgan," I pointed out, even though I had since learned that Andrew Morgan's real name was Arthur Dieppe. "And nobody knows it was Jake. There's no proof."

"Right," Ross said, but he meant the opposite. "Right. Let's see: Guy with a criminal past — "

"He was a kid, Ross."

"Kids grow up," Ross said. "And he grew up to be a guy with a criminal past, a violent temper — which practically everyone at school has seen — a history of hanging around with the wrong crowd, a guy who was extremely jealous because his girl-friend was seeing someone else, and who has no alibi for the night of the murder. Gosh," he said, pretending to be breaking his brain trying to assemble the puzzle he had laid out, "who could possibly have killed Tessa?"

"History, Ross," I said. "What you're saying is ancient history. Jake did some things he shouldn't have when he was a kid. So what? And he wasn't hanging around with the wrong crowd anymore — "

"But he *was* jealous," Ross said. I think he enjoyed saying it. I think it made him feel important. "He was jealous because Tessa was seeing me. And because of that and because of his temper, Tessa was afraid of him."

I looked at Ross. My friend. He was smart in a lot of ways. He was good at his job as editor of the East Hastings *Herald*. He did well in school. There was no doubt in my mind that he would make it to law school. He would probably graduate at the head of his class and, given his suspicious nature, would end up working as a Crown attorney. But there were some things he didn't understand, and those things made him blind to what was really happening. That blindness wasn't helping him now, and for sure it wouldn't help him later on. Someone had to set him straight. Because he was my friend and because I was getting tired of his groundless declarations, I decided to be the one to do it.

"She wasn't interested in going out with you," I told my friend. "She was using you."

At first his head snapped back a little, as if he were dodging a slap. Then it went red, the way it might have if the slap had landed.

"She wasn't using me," he said. "Tessa wasn't like that."

"I don't mean she was using you in a mean way," I said. I was pretty sure that was true. "She was using you to get information. You told me so yourself." So had Jake. "She was asking questions about me and about Levesque. She wanted to know what he was like."

"So?"

"So, she knew that you and I are friends," I said. "And she knew that you know Levesque."

"She wasn't using me. She liked me. She was nice to me."

"I'm sure she was, but — "

"And she was angry with Jake. They were fighting all the time."

"Did she tell you why?" Jake had said it was because he didn't have enough ambition.

"Not exactly," Ross said angrily. "Not in so many words. But she didn't have to tell me. It was obvious. As I believe I have mentioned on more than one occasion, Jake didn't want her to spend time with me. Jake has a bad temper. And — maybe you haven't been listening — Jake hangs around with all the wrong people."

"Not anymore." Maybe I should have shouted the words at him. Maybe then he would have heard them.

"Then why did she blame him for Danny?"

Danny? "What about Danny?"

"Danny thought Jake was really cool. It was because of Jake that Danny got involved with Marcus and Jordan. That bothered Tessa a lot."

"Tessa was mad at Jake because Jake got Danny involved with Marcus and his gang? Is that what you're saying?"

"It was one of the reasons," Ross said.

"Did she tell you that?"

He gave me a look. "She didn't have to," he said. "It was obvious. Everyone knew."

Everyone except me.

* * *

I found Jake in the garage beside his house. He was peering under the hood of a car that looked old enough to be my mother. He didn't hear me coming, and because I was afraid he'd do one of those classic cartoon bonk-the-head-on-the-upraised-hood movements if I cleared my throat or made any other sudden noise, I waited. After a few moments, he straightened up. He noticed me before I could announce myself and was so startled he did one of those classic cartoon drop-the-heavy-wrench-on-the-toe-of-his-sneaker things. This was followed by a shout and a lot of hopping around on his part.

"Sorry," I said.

He glowered at me. "What do you want?"

"It wasn't Andrew Morgan," I said. "He was in jail in Sudbury the night Tessa died."

Jake's eyes narrowed. "So, what does that mean? That now you think it was me after all?"

"I didn't say that."

"What, then?"

"You used to hang out with Marcus and Jordan, right?"

He looked even more suspicious now. "Yeah, so? In case you haven't noticed, I don't do that anymore."

"You got Danny involved with them, right?"

He bent down to retrieve the fallen wrench.

When he stood up again it was clutched tightly in his hands. It looked like it could be an effective weapon, if he wanted to use it that way.

"I didn't get Danny involved in anything. Danny got himself involved. He started hanging around with those guys. I told him it was stupid. Besides, he didn't have any excuses."

"What do you mean?"

"Before I even moved here, I knew a guy who knew Marcus." I didn't know for sure and he didn't say, but I guessed it had something to do with the group home he had spent time in. "When we moved here, Marcus had already heard about me from this guy. He introduced himself to me the first day I was at school and he seemed okay, you know?" I didn't. He shrugged. "It wasn't like I knew a million people up here. So, okay, I started hanging out with him and Jordan and the rest of them. But Danny knew everyone here, so he had no excuse. He was just stupid. He just thought those guys were something special. I told him he was wrong, but he wouldn't listen. Tessa and I almost split up over the whole thing."

"When was that?"

"Eight, nine months ago. She got all mad at me because Danny decided to be a loser like those guys. I wasn't involved with them anymore, so I didn't see why she was mad at me. I told her, Danny's a big boy. He's old enough to make his own mistakes. He doesn't need my help."

"And?"

"And what?"

"How did Tessa take that?"

"She got over it."

I waited.

"Okay," he exploded at last. "So maybe he got the idea from me that those guys were something special. But they're not. I cut loose, and I told him if he was smart, he'd do the same thing. But he didn't listen. I'm sorry about that. But it wasn't my fault."

"What do they do?"

"What do who do?"

"Marcus and his bunch? What's their claim to fame?"

"Besides stupidity, you mean?" Jake shook his head. "A year ago, they just had attitude. You know, cutting class. Smoking. Playing a little mailbox baseball out on the concession roads." When I gave him a blank look, he explained. "That's where you and your favorite baseball bat get into a car and see how many roadside mailboxes you can decimate without stopping the car or even slowing down."

"Fun," I said.

"Stupid," he said. "'Course, I didn't always think so."

"You said that's what they were doing a year ago. What about lately?"

Jake shrugged. "I bailed out when they started ganging up on kids, demanding money and smokes. I don't know what they're up to now. But I'll tell you something — that Jordan is nuts. He's going to end up in jail one of these days."

"You think maybe Danny's been trying to quit them and that's why he and Jordan are fighting all the time?"

Jake frowned. "What do you mean?"

"I mean, do you think Danny maybe decided to listen to his sister after all and get out of the gang?"

Jake waved his hand impatiently. "What do you mean, they're fighting all the time?"

I reminded him about what had happened up in the park after Tessa's funeral. He looked blankly at me.

"I wasn't exactly tuned into the world then," he said.

Then I told him about what had happened at Winterfoot when Jordan had tried to steal the money from the waffle stand. And as I was telling him, I remembered what had happened when I had gone over to see Danny, how he had been listening to me right up until Marcus and Jordan showed up, and then how he had gotten mad at me and had shoved me away.

Jake shrugged. "If they've been fighting like that in public, then something's happening," he said. "It's usually one hundred percent solidarity with those guys. They stick together no matter what. The only time I ever saw them fight — correction, the only time Marcus ever allowed a fight — was just before I bailed."

"What happened?"

"Marcus and Jordan had this idea how they could make themselves some extra cash."

I waited.

"A lot of the younger kids think they're cool," Jake said. "A lot of kids want to hang out with them. Marcus had this idea he could get these kids to do a little borrowing for him."

"Borrowing?"

"From stores. You know, steal stuff that could be sold for extra money. I told them no way. First of all, if they wanted to take stuff, they should do it themselves and not get younger kids to do it for them. Second, I told them if they started doing that, I was out. Fact is, I had more or less decided to get out anyway. I thought what they were doing was pretty stupid. I'd had enough trouble. I wanted something different." He gave me an odd little smile. "I guess you could say Tessa had something to do with that. She made me think maybe I could get through school okay. Maybe I could do something with my life."

"What happened?"

He sighed. "I was up in Morrisville with Marcus and Jordan. We were in a store up there. We were looking around and I felt something. I had on a backpack — we had hitched up there and I had brought some sandwiches and chips. Those guys always had lots of money for food, but I never did. Anyway, I felt something. Jordan was standing behind me trying to look all innocent, like he had just jostled me or something. He apologized. You know, sorry, man. Then we were heading for the door and, I don't even know why, I just got this feeling. I started to take off my backpack. Then Jordan is saying, 'Come on, man, we've got to get out of here if we're going to catch a ride while it's still light, while people are still going to be stopping.' That's when I knew something was up. I took off the backpack and I saw he had shoved a bunch of CDs into it and I went nuts. Idiot! You have to have the brains of a mosquito not to know the CDs are all tagged for security. I would have gotten caught for sure. I ditched the stuff and when we got out of the store, I started swinging at him. Marcus just stood there and watched." He sighed. "I got the worst of that fight. Later, I tried to explain to Marcus what a jerk Jordan had been, and you know what he said to me?"

I had no idea.

"He said, 'Seems to me your heart isn't in this, Jake. Seems to me ever since you started seeing that girl' — he meant Tessa — 'you forgot who your friends are.'"

"He knew what Jordan was doing?"

Jake snorted. "Are you kidding? Marcus probably put him up to it. I wouldn't go along with them, so they were going to get me nailed for shoplifting. That's when I dumped them. I thought they'd give me a hard time, but they didn't. The next thing I knew, Danny had taken up with them and Tessa was all mad at me."

"What do you think it means, Danny and Jordan

fighting?"

Jake's smile was crooked. "Sounds to me like maybe there's trouble in paradise."

"You think maybe Danny wants out?"

"If he does, he never said anything to me."

"What about Tessa?"

"What about her?"

"Did she say anything to you?"

"Other than all of a sudden deciding that I was wasting my life?" He shook his head. "No. She didn't."

* * *

I thought about Tessa and Danny as I trudged down the road from Jake's house to town. Fact: A couple of weeks before she died, Tessa had started getting on Jake's case about the people he used to hang out with and the plans, or lack of plans, he had for his life. Fact: Tessa had been asking a lot of questions about me and Levesque. Fact: Tessa had showed up at our house looking for Levesque, but even after I told her she would have better luck finding him at the police station, she hadn't gone there and hadn't talked to him. Fact: Tessa had been scared of someone and afraid that someone was following her. Fact: Danny Nixon had had some kind of falling out with his gang, but something was stopping him from making a complete break with them. Fact: Danny acted one way when his gang was around and another way when it wasn't. Fact: There was a thread that linked all of these things. Okay, so maybe the last fact wasn't a fact after all. Maybe it was just a theory. But I was sure there was a link.

The walk took a little over an hour, and between the time I left Jake's place and the time I caught sight of Centre Street, the temperature had dropped again and it had started to snow. Snow! It was over halfway through March. Who wanted to think about shoveling snow when April showers were just around the corner?

I wasn't planning to go to the police station. At least, I wasn't planning it when I left Jake's house. But by the time I reached town, two things had happened. One, my feet were freezing. The boots I was wearing looked great, but they were designed for city, not country, living. Between the time I left Jake's and the time I got close to town, there were two or three more inches of snow on the ground. Two, Danny Nixon was eating at me. Something must have happened a few weeks before Tessa died. There must have been some type of falling out with the gang. Maybe Tessa had gotten wind of it. Maybe she had been thinking about doing something about it so that she could get her brother away from them once and for all. But what had happened?

That clinched it. I started to walk a little faster, and I don't think anyone was ever happier to walk through the front door of a police station than I was that afternoon. When it turned out that the only person there was Steve Denby, I couldn't decide whether I was relieved or disappointed.

Steve smiled right up until he saw my stylish,

181

but very wet, boots and the puddles they were making on the floor.

"Ski-doo boots are your best bet up here in winter," he said.

"Officially," I pointed out, "it's almost spring."

He laughed, while I looked around.

"He isn't here," Steve said.

"Oh." I tried to sound disappointed.

"Anything I can help you with?"

I chewed on my lip so that it looked like I was agonizing over the question. "Well . . . " I said. Then, "Never mind."

If I were an angler and Steve were a trout, I'd be looking at a fish fry tonight.

"What?" he said.

"Lev— Louis promised to help me with an assignment for my civics class." Okay, so that wasn't exactly true. But one thing experience had taught me since moving up here was that adults just love to hear how much kids are learning in school. The only thing they like better is the thought that somehow they can contribute to the educational experience. And when experience teaches you that something is true and it works, well, who am I, a mere mortal, to argue? "He said he'd be here."

Like every other adult I have ever tried this on, Steve perked up at the prospect of being helpful.

"Maybe there's something I can do," he said. "I've lived here all my life. If you have any questions about civics in East Hastings, I'm your man."

Still I hesitated, giving, I hoped, the impression

182

of someone who was reluctant to impose on someone else's good nature.

"He was going to help me find out what was happening around here a couple of weeks ago," I said.

"What was happening?" Steve sounded baffled.

"Complaint-wise. My civics teacher wants us to put together a day-in-the-life-of-the-town project. Guess what I got assigned?" I shook my head and did my best to sound disgusted, even though I didn't even take civics. Steve didn't know that, though. "Everyone thinks that because my stepdad is a cop, I know everything there is to know about crime patterns and crime rates. Like I even care! On the other hand, it's an easy term mark. The thing is, I have to pull it all together for the day after tomorrow."

Steve's smile had long-since faded. "You know how your stepdad feels about police business," he said.

I made a face. "You mean, have I heard the lecture about ten million times? You know I have. But he promised to help me. All I want to know is what kind of crimes happen in town in a typical two-to-three-week period? I don't want to know who, just what kind and how many. How many drunk and disorderlies, how many break and enters, how many public mischiefs, that kind of thing. Crime stats." When he still looked reluctant, I said, "It's okay, though. If he's not here like he said he was going to be — "

"It's not his fault. Something came up," Steve said.

"Yeah. Right. Well, it's not like I haven't heard

that before. I just hope my teacher buys it." I stomped my feet and turned to the door.

"For sure he said he was going to help you with this?" Steve said.

I turned, a look of deep hurt on my face. "For sure," I said. "But it's okay. It's not a big deal. So I lose ten points for being late — "

Steve sighed. "Okay. Just stats, right?"

"Right," I said. "No names. Just numbers."

He headed for the files. I followed him.

Chapter 15

Twenty minutes later, I was forming a whole new — and much more dismal — view of the town I now called home. In late January and early February, a month to six weeks before Tessa had died, the following charges had been laid in East Hastings:

Three people were charged with assault. Apparently they had assaulted each other at a local bar. Something about a bet on a hockey game.

One person broke a window at the liquor store after hours. He didn't get inside, though, because the alarm went off, and the liquor store is all of a block away from the police station.

Someone else was charged for taking a swing at another person who had supposedly stolen his parking spot in front of the drugstore. In February. Not exactly the height of the tourist season. Not a time of year when parking is a problem in East Hastings.

A man was given a warning after making a series of nuisance phone calls, twenty-seven in all, to another person, who happened to be his brother. It was another case of a bet on a hockey game — this one an unpaid bet. I wondered if it was connected to the triple assault at the bar.

Two people — cousins — were arrested for shooting a deer out of season.

A woman was charged with theft after taking a stack of old magazines out of the local dentist's office. The magazines were so old, the woman said, that she had thought they were being discarded. She had wanted to clip recipes out of them. The dentist later withdrew his complaint. He had been annoyed because the woman had a large dental bill outstanding.

"And then there's that convenience store hold-up," Steve said.

East Hastings' one and only unsolved crime, up until Tessa was murdered.

"The chief is up at the hospital in Morrisville right now," Steve said. "That clerk who was shot is making a slow recovery. The chief keeps hoping he'll remember something helpful."

According to what I had read in the local paper, the clerk had been whacked pretty hard over the head with something reported to be a length of steel pipe. I wondered what shape his brain was in, let alone his memory. The only other person in the store at the time was the owner, and he had been killed. According to the local paper, he had been shot with his own gun. The police hadn't found any fingerprints. The store had a surveillance camera, but it hadn't been operational. Apparently it was only for show. There had been no tire tracks, no useful footprints, nothing. No one had seen any-thing — the convenience store was conveniently located in an out-of-the-way spot.

"That's about it," Steve said. He shoved the last

of the files back into the file drawer just as the phone rang. He reached across his desk to answer it, and almost jumped to attention when whoever was on the other end started talking. It didn't take much to figure out who that someone was. I grabbed my coat, pulled it on and started for the door.

"Any luck?" Steve was saying. Then, "That's all, huh? You think maybe he'll be able to remember anything else?" Pause. "Yeah, well, we can always hope, I guess." Then he laid a hand over the mouthpiece and called to me, "You want to talk to your stepdad?"

I shook my head and mouthed, "Gotta run."

As I opened the door I heard Steve say, "By the way, I took care of that project you were supposed to help Chloe with — " I shut the door quickly behind me so I wouldn't have to see poor Steve try to explain exactly what the project was.

* * *

While I was in the station house, the snow on my pretty city boots melted and soaked right through. Within minutes of being outside again, my wet boots and socks started to harden and my feet started to freeze. I decided to take a shortcut home.

The snow was coming down steadily in large, lacy flakes. It was all as pretty as a Christmas card, except that Christmas was by now a distant memory. I headed away from Centre Street and made my way along the railroad tracks. If I cut across the tracks at the level crossing — my mother would have had a heart attack if she knew what I was thinking — I could shave a good ten minutes off my walk. Maybe that way I would get home before my feet turned into blocks of ice.

As I trudged along I tried not to think about Levesque's reaction to what Steve Denby had told him about my project. That's tried not to think as in, try not to think of a five-hundred-pound pink canary in a frilly tutu dancing *Swan Lake*. You can't help but conjure up a picture of what you're supposed to be trying *not* to think about. Levesque was going to be angry, that was for sure. There was a chance that I could deflect his anger with the theory I had kicking around my brain. I wasn't one hundred percent positive about it, but if I were Levesque, assuming I wasn't blinded by anger, I would at least give a quick listen to what I had to say, especially if I could demonstrate a link between two major and, so far, unsolved crimes. In fact . . .

I stopped suddenly and spun around.

Nothing.

Nothing except a feeling. Snow was falling so fast and thick that it seemed to curtain the world. I saw no one and nothing except pure whiteness. At the same time, everything had gone still. There was no wind, not even a breeze. The snow was coming down straight and heavy. It muffled all sound except the perfect silence of each flake landing on trees, on hedges, on the ground. It almost seemed too quiet.

I turned and started walking again, but I just couldn't fight the feeling that someone was out there, and that whoever that someone was, they were watching me. I stopped again, and turned to look behind me.

Nothing. No one.

But when I turned again to continue walking, I broke the silence with a gasp of surprise. Someone was coming out of the snow toward me as if he were appearing from a thick mist. It was Danny Nixon. Something was dangling from one of his hands. As he drew closer I saw that he had that same weird unfocused look that he'd had when I had found him standing outside my house. Pretty soon I could smell the sourness on his breath. I saw that he was holding a tire iron.

"Hi," he said.

"Hi, Danny." I tried hard to keep the nervous quiver from my voice, but I don't think he noticed either way. He wasn't even looking at me. Instead, he was looking someplace over my shoulder.

"I'm sorry," he said.

"Sorry for what?"

He nodded behind me. I turned. Marcus Tyrell and Jordan and a couple of the others were coming out of the snow toward me. Jordan was smiling. It wasn't the kind of smile that made a person feel welcome. Just the opposite. He came up close to me. Too close.

"Well, hello there," he said. Then, yuck, he reached out to touch my face. I pulled back, and felt a pair of arms close around my middle. I didn't know who was behind me — maybe Danny, maybe one of the others — but whoever it was, he let out a yelp and dropped his arms when I stomped down hard on one of his feet. He tried to grab me again, but I managed to wriggle clear of him. Not that it helped me much. They had closed in a circle around me. There were six of them, including Danny. Six of them and one of me.

"You'd better leave me alone," I said. Before I even finished saying the words, I knew what they were all thinking: Or what? "Look, my dad is chief of police." I focused on Marcus Tyrell. He was the leader of the group. He called the shots. The others went along with whatever he said. "You guys don't want the grief of having to deal with him. And, trust me, if you guys bother me, if you hurt me, you will definitely have to deal with him."

"Oooooh, I'm scared," Jordan said, making an exaggerated, clownish attempt to look nervous. Then he stepped inside the circle that had formed around me. The others closed the gap he had left, and Jordan reached out for me again. I slapped his hand away. The smile vanished from his face. Then, before I realized what was happening, he hit me, hard enough to make tears come to my eyes. I wiped them away angrily. Tears would make it look like I was crying, and a crying girl always made a guy think of weakness. That was the last thing I wanted these guys to think. I decided to give my theory a try, just to see if it had any validation . . .

and if it did, whether it would make these jerks back off.

"That clerk from the convenience store is getting better," I told them. I was shaking all over now, and it wasn't just because my feet were freezing. We were down near the railway tracks where, unless a train went by in the next couple of minutes, no one could see me, which meant that no one could help me. "When he does, the cops will be all over you."

I saw Marcus Tyrell's face harden and realized two things. One: My theory was right. Two: I had said the wrong thing. I had just told them that I knew they were responsible for the convenience store holdup. I had also told them that the police didn't know that yet. Stupid, stupid, stupid.

Marcus nodded at Danny.

Danny started to move in toward me.

"Hey, I can handle this," Jordan said. Out came his hand again, only this time he succeeded in grabbing one of my cheeks. He pinched it hard. When I swung out a hand to hit him, someone behind me grabbed it and wrenched it. I cried out. I couldn't help it, it hurt.

"Danny does this one," Marcus said. "It's his big mouth that caused this trouble in the first place. It's his sister that went over to the cop's house and got Chloe here into it. Isn't that right, Danny?" I noticed that he talked softly, but everyone heard him. They all hung on his words.

I spun around to look at Danny. Someone grabbed me from behind. Then Marcus came up in front of me. He was smiling. He grabbed the front of my jacket and unzipped it. I tried to stop him — whatever he was planning, I knew I wasn't going to like it — but whoever had hold of me from behind had a tight grip. Then someone else ripped off my jacket. I started to shiver. Then I started to panic. I was out in the middle of a snowstorm in just my shirt and my jeans, surrounded by half a dozen guys who didn't look friendly and sure weren't acting friendly, and there was no one around to help me. My feet, already wet, were starting to feel like blocks of ice. Without my jacket, my body temperature would start to drop. I had a feeling, though, that hypothermia was going to be the least of my problems.

"Come on," Marcus said. "Let's get her out of here."

Someone — Jordan, I think — shoved me from behind.

"The car's that way," he said, nodding up the tracks, away from town. There wasn't much up there — a side road that didn't get much traffic, a railway trestle, the edge of the park.

I started walking. I was shaking with cold. And with fear. I had to get away from them before they got me to their car, because once they had me there, they could take me anywhere and do their best to see that I didn't get home again. I looked around to see what my chances were. Not good, I figured. Not with six of them. Not with them fanned out around me, ready to stop me if I decided to run. Jordan jabbed me from behind to make me walk faster.

I looked at Danny, who was walking beside me, the tire iron gripped in his gloved hand, ready to swing. Unlike the others, he didn't seem to be enjoying himself.

"You guys killed Tessa because she found out what happened, right?" I said. I kept my voice low and tried to hold it steady. I wanted him to know I was talking to him and him alone. I also wanted to give him the impression that I wasn't afraid.

He didn't say anything.

"She found out what you did, and you killed her because she was going to go to the cops," I said. My teeth were chattering like one of those wind-up toys.

Danny remained silent.

"Everyone said you and Tessa were close," I said. "Guess that shows that everybody isn't always so brilliant." That last part I sort of muttered to myself. "What now, Danny? You guys going to kill me, too, just like you killed Tessa? Am I ever glad I don't have any brothers."

Danny Nixon glanced around at his friends. When he spoke, his voice was quiet. "I never touched Tessa," he hissed.

"Yeah, right."

He glowered at me. The tire iron jumped in his hand and I cringed, afraid he was going to swing it at me.

"It was them," he said. "They killed that guy at the store, and when Tessa found out and wanted to

193

go to the cops, they . . . "

I finished his sentence for him. "They killed her?" He gave a nod, just a tiny one, but I knew it meant yes.

"And you let them?"

He shook his head, as if he were trying to remember something. "She figured out something was wrong. She always knew when something was going on with me. She thought she could get me away from those guys and out of trouble. She was always trying to help me, whether I wanted her to or not." His eyes weren't focusing properly. I wondered how much he'd had to drink to try to make himself forget what he and his friends had done.

"And now you're trying to help yourself, right?" I said. I was so cold I was starting to feel warm, which I knew was not a good sign. I was angry, too. Danny Nixon had stood silent while his so-called friends killed his sister. And now he was getting ready to hurt me, permanently. "Do unto me what your pals did unto Tessa, eh? Your very own interpretation of the Golden Rule."

Danny glanced at his friends again.

"You don't understand," Danny said. It came out like a whisper. "I have to do it. I have no choice. I betrayed these guys when I told Tessa . . . "

Wait a minute! *He* had told Tessa what had happened at the convenience store? Why would he have done that? Why would he have told *anyone* what had happened? My mind was racing, trying to figure out what that meant. Maybe Danny had actually been looking for help, for some way out.

"If I don't do what they tell me now," Danny said, "they're going to do the same thing to me that they did to Tessa."

"Nice friends," I said.

"It has nothing to do with friendship anymore," Danny said.

Up ahead I saw a battered old gas-guzzler of a car. If I got into that car, I'd be going on the ride of a lifetime. Danny was my only chance — if he was still looking for a way out.

"Tessa seemed to think you were worth something," I said. "She put her life on the line to help you. And for what? Turns out she was wrong. Turns out you aren't worth anything at all. You're just like them. You just let it happen. You let that man get killed at the convenience store and you let your own sister get killed to cover it up. I didn't know Tessa well, but I sure am sorry she had to die for a piece of garbage like you."

Danny turned on me. All of a sudden he seemed to have no trouble holding me in clear focus.

"I didn't know," he said. "I didn't know what they had done until after they had done it, and then they told me if I said anything, I'd be next."

"And now they want you to take care of me so you'll be just like them — a murderer. Then you'll never be able to do the right thing, will you, Danny? You'll have the perfect excuse to go on being a piece of garbage just like your friends, because they'll have something to hold over you for the rest of your life."

We were only steps from the car now, and the rest of the gang was starting to close around us. Danny turned and looked at me. Some kind of war was being waged on his face. Then, suddenly, he shoved me, hard.

"Go," he said. "Now! Run!"

He didn't have to tell me twice. My feet were almost frozen solid and I was shaking so hard my teeth hurt, but I ran. I ran and I didn't look back. If they were chasing me, I didn't want to know. If they were gaining on me, I definitely didn't want to know. Then I felt a hand grab me and jerk me back. I whirled around. My arm felt like it was being ripped out of its socket. Jordan sneered at me. Then, suddenly, his face went blank and he collapsed in a heap at my feet. Danny stood over him, staring down at the tire iron in his hand. I saw the rest of them coming and I turned and ran again. This time I did glance back. Danny was doing his best to hold them off, but he was badly outnumbered. I didn't see how he was going to succeed.

I did the only thing I could. I kept on running.

I had just hit one of the side streets that led to Centre Street when I was grabbed again. This time the hands were bigger and stronger. Levesque. I saw the police car in the middle of the road, the driver's side door still open. He must have seen me coming. He took his coat off and wrapped it around me. Then he made me sit in the car while I blurted out my story. He radioed Steve Denby, who appeared on the run a moment later. He was wearing only street shoes and was pulling on his coat.

"Okay," Levesque said. "Show us where."

They had all vanished by the time we got there. All except Danny Nixon, who was lying on the ground. The tire iron, one end covered in blood, lay beside him, under a thin blanket of big, lacy snowflakes. Levesque knelt beside him.

"He's still breathing," he said to Steve Denby. "Call Emergency."

I had warmed up a little, thanks to Levesque's sheepskin jacket, but, looking at Danny, I started to shiver all over again. I was still shivering an hour later when I was safely under my quilt and filled with hot tea.

Chapter 16

I didn't wake up until nearly noon the next day, and that surprised me. After what had happened, I hadn't expected to get any sleep at all. What surprised me more was that both my mother and Levesque were in the kitchen when I padded downstairs to make myself a cup of tea.

Mom sprang up immediately and came at me with the flat of her hand ready to lay against my forehead.

"I'm fine, Mom," I said. "I'm not sick."

Both arms went out then and she wrapped me in a great big hug.

"Are you okay, Mom?" I asked.

She snuffled. Good old Mom.

"Sit down," she said. "I'll make you some breakfast."

I sat at the table. Levesque's big hands were wrapped around a mug of coffee. While Mom scurried around, getting eggs and butter out of the fridge and bread out of the breadbox, he sipped his coffee. After a little, I couldn't hold back anymore, I had to ask. "How's Danny?"

He didn't say anything right away. Instead, he took a sip of his coffee.

"Come on, I was there," I said. "If anything bad happened to him, it was because he was trying to help me. I have a right to know whether he's okay."

"Danny's going to be fine. He has a hairline fracture

and needed a few stitches, but he'll definitely live."

The next question was a little more of a problem, because it would take me straight into Official Police Investigation territory.

"I know I'm not supposed to ask," I said, "and I know you told me you didn't want to hear me mention Tessa's name — "

Bingo, there it was, that twitching underneath his bushy moustache. He was smiling. Smiling was good. As good as a green light.

"Did Danny tell you anything?" I asked.

Levesque nodded. "He told us everything."

I waited, holding my tongue, and was, for once, rewarded for my patience.

"He got in way over his head with that bunch," Levesque said. "The convenience store robbery really scared him."

"He told Tessa about it."

Levesque nodded. "I know. And she tried to convince him to go to the police. Finally she told him if he didn't, *she* would. When word got back to the rest of the gang . . . " He shrugged, as if the rest of the story were self-evident.

"But how?" Tessa wouldn't have let anything slip. Neither would Danny, at least, not intentionally. "How did they know?"

"Danny says the robbery really jangled him. He thinks the rest of the gang started to worry about him. They kept a pretty close watch on him. He's not one hundred percent sure exactly when it happened, but he says that at least on one occasion when Tessa was arguing with him, Jordan and Marcus could have overheard something. Danny told them not to worry about Tessa, but they must have decided to keep an eye on her."

"You mean, they were watching her?"

"Danny says he thinks they were following her."

No wonder she had been so nervous when she came here. Maybe that also explained why she hadn't gone directly to the police station. There isn't much that happens on Centre Street that doesn't draw the attention of at least half the population of East Hastings.

"And they killed her to stop her from telling you anything?"

Levesque nodded.

"Do you know who actually did it?"

"I know who Danny said it was."

I wished I were standing at a roulette table at one of those big casinos in Las Vegas, and I wished I had a million dollars to play because I knew exactly what number the little white ball was going to hit.

"It was Jordan, wasn't it?"

"That's what Danny alleges — "

"It was Jordan," I said, and shuddered.

Levesque glanced over at my mother, who looked back with a worried expression on her face.

"Did they hurt you?" Levesque said. He was watching me closely. "Because if they did . . . "

"They didn't hurt me," I said. "They scared me, but they didn't hurt me. They would have, though, if Danny hadn't decided to help me."

"You're sure they didn't hurt you?"

I nodded. If you measured hurt by the bruises and scars you could see, they hadn't hurt me.

Jake showed up on my doorstep later that afternoon. I was home alone — well, alone with Shendor — when he rang the bell, and when I went to answer it, he stepped way back from the door.

"Come in," I said.

"No, it's okay," he said, and stepped back another pace. One more and he'd fall right down the steps. "I heard what happened and I just wanted to make sure you were okay."

"So, come in and see for yourself." He didn't move. "Oh, for heaven's sake," I said, and went out onto the porch in my slippers and grabbed him by the arm and brought him inside. I shoved him ahead of me into the kitchen. "Sit," I said. "You like tea?" He shrugged. I put the kettle on to boil. Then I said, "I owe you an apology."

"I think it's the other way around," Jake said. "I think I owe you an apology."

That was a big surprise. "I owe you one because for a while there, I really thought you might have done it," I said.

"Yeah, well, I owe you one because for a whole lot longer than a minute, I thought you were a real pain in the butt."

I smiled at him. Then I started to laugh.

"Apology accepted," I said.

"Me, too."

The kettle started to screech. I poured boiling

water over the two teabags in Mom's big brown teapot. I was just getting the milk out of the fridge when the doorbell rang again. I left Jake in the kitchen and went to answer it.

"Ross!"

He brought his hand out from behind his back and produced a cone of paper. Flowers, I guessed.

"For you," he said. "I heard what happened. I owe you an apology."

I couldn't help it. I started to laugh again.

"What?" Ross said.

"Come in."

"What's so funny?" His eyes narrowed. "Okay, I get it. You were right and I was wrong. I admit it. You were right. That's why I came over here. That plus the fact that I wasn't very nice to you the last time I saw you. And then the next thing I hear is that you almost got yourself killed — "

I grabbed him by the arm and pulled him inside.

"I just made tea," I said. "You want to join us?"

"Us?"

I pulled him into the kitchen. Puzzlement left his face at about the same time a look of nasty surprise settled on it.

"You know Jake, don't you, Ross?" I said. I kept my voice light, like a perky hostess who was just trying to make sure that everyone felt comfortable around everyone else.

Jake looked at Ross in pretty much the same way that Ross was looking at Jake. They were like two stray, streetwise mutts, sniffing each other out.

"Jake was just telling me what a pain in the butt he thought I was," I said to Ross, "so I know you two have at least one thing in common. Sit down, Ross."

He stayed standing. I had to push him down into a chair.

"You know," I said, as I poured a cup of tea for each of them, "I got the impression from Danny Nixon that Tessa was someone really special. She put her life on the line for him. How many people would do something like that? I sure wish I had gotten to know her better."

I poured some tea for myself and sat down. Jake was staring down into his cup. Ross was stirring sugar into his. Stirring and stirring and stirring.

"She told me you were a good friend," Jake said at last. He wasn't looking at me. He was looking at Ross. Ross stared at him, open-mouthed. "She told me that she'd known you practically her whole life and that when you guys were younger, you used to hang out all the time."

Ross set down the spoon. He looked at me and then he looked at Jake.

"I miss her," he said finally.

"So do I," Jake said.

"Tell me about her, would you?" I prodded gently.

And then there we were, three people sitting around talking about someone one of us hadn't known very well and two of us had loved very much. By the end, I really did wish I had gotten to know Tessa Nixon. She sounded like an angel.

Introduction

t o many, the good old days never seemed better than they do now. How assuring it was to have that big, solid structure of the Church behind us, protecting us from the cradle to the grave.

The Church had clear answers to almost all questions, definite rules for getting to heaven, and crackling good warning signs along the broad way to hell.

But now, some Catholics feel that the Rock of Peter is being engulfed in quicksand. "Nothing is a sin anymore." The "love bit" has taken over. Now you can "form your own conscience" and everybody is right, nobody is wrong.

Others, probably most of us over 30, will readily admit that some of the things we learned in grade school were a little unrealistic. We see the need for updating and have picked up bits and pieces of the new thinking about the Commandments, but would appreciate a clear overview. Those of us under 30 are just interested in a clear statement in today's terms of Christian moral teachings. All of us, no matter what our fears or age or temperament, see the need to understand how others — our parents, children, co-workers, friends — reach their moral positions.

It may be small comfort to those who feel burned by the explosion of change, but the Church has been through the anguish of growth before. Back in the fourth century, the emperor Constantine brought the Church up out of the catacombs and made it *the* religion of the empire. Many people must have started looking back to the good old days when it *cost* something to be a Christian, when the Church bore the marks of the poor and suffering Christ instead of lounging about in imperial robes.

And in the 13th century at least a great many of the clergy must have been disturbed no end when a certain "way-out" theologian named Aquinas upset all theology by going back to that infernal pagan Greek Aristotle for guidance.

Galileo destroyed some good old days too, moving our cozy world from the center of the stage. Some of his friends wouldn't look into his telescope.

Many probably felt it was a step backward when the popes lost their temporal power and no longer crowned the successors of Constantine.

And so on down to our own day, when both Protestant and Catholic and Jewish Bible scholars explain that the inspired writers meant far less — and far more — than we thought they did; when psychologists explore the depths of the human person and decide that human conduct is woven of many strands, many of them not visible; when sociologists opine that not all that Churches do is the result of religious motivation, and when scientists probe to the roots of matter itself.

We might hope that this would all go away, runs the anguished comment of some parents, but the worst of the bad things is that all this confusion is being poured into our children's heads by a religious education philosophy that is mushy at best and heretical at worst.

Who's to blame? Parents blame teachers (especially those long-suffering servants of the Church, the high-school religion departments). Teachers blame permissive parents. Parents and teachers blame priests and nuns. Priests blame theologians, and everybody blames the bishops, the Pope (either John or Paul) or Vatican II. Young people shake their heads at all the bickering.

Won't somebody please turn off the bubble machine?

All of us may as well accept that the untidy confusing, uncertain aspects of morality are not going to go away. The reason is, to make a long story short, that life itself is a "mess"; that's what makes it worth living — mysterious, challenging, open to endless possibilities. That's the way God made it. It has as many loose ends as tight ones, as many unmarked paths as well-lighted highways. Since morality has to do with life in all its aspects, morality will be just as complex as life. The surprising thing is that we could have imagined it to be otherwise.

The trouble was (to oversimplify) that we paid too much attention to the package and not enough to the contents. We thought that everything could have a very legible label of "good" or "bad." Every moral question had a trumpet-like "Yes!" or "No!" answer.

Values were presupposed, often not discussed. We worried about the *laws* that were to promote and protect *values* more than we did about the values themselves. How many of us, for instance, could identify the positive values of being chaste as well as we could list the ways of being unchaste?

The new approach in morality says that it is not enough merely to do the externally good thing and avoid the externally bad thing. It is not enough to keep specific laws: there are laws, but beyond that there are positive *values* that must be sought in all moral decisions and practice.

Values are complex and interrelated. Personal motivation is an ongoing, unmeasurable affair; the "law" of love still calls us when all the other laws have been kept. Hence the apparent haziness and "messiness" of a morality that involves what is deeply inside the human person, while not discounting his external actions.

In this book we hope to show that morality must be rooted in the Gospel. The goodness or badness of Christian living must be estimated not only in terms of the Ten Commandments, but above all in terms of the Two Great Commandments: "This is the greatest and the first commandment: you shall love the Lord your God with your whole heart; the second is like it: you shall love your neighbor as yourself" — and finally in terms of the primary Christian call: *to live and love as Jesus did.*

The present days (whether they become the "good old" or not) challenge us to live the Gospel of Jesus in our circumstances, in the complexity and search for value that our new exploding culture has forced upon us. The time has come not to despair but to accept the challenge of discovering in a deeper and fuller way what Christian morality is all about.

People in other vocations obviously do not have the time and opportunity to read and research as professional theologians do. But they have the need and the right to know, and theologians have the duty and privilege of sharing the fruits of their labors. Theologians can help others to search, and in turn be helped by the insights and wisdom of men and women who deal more directly with life than with books and ideas.

This book is an attempt to share insights, such as they are, that have come through much struggle and reading and teaching.

It is divided into two parts. Part I tries to make clear the values and ingredients of all morality; what the presuppositions are that blaze the path for all Christian behavior, as well as all laws, general or specific. Part II searches for the values God wishes us to achieve in giving us the Ten Commandments and the Basic Two.

May it bring all of us closer to him who is our Life and Light and unchanging Hope.

Part One:
THE PEOPLE
JESUS HAS
IN MIND